MW01145492

Printed in the United States
137562LV00002B/11/P

9 780981 688343

SIX YEARS
MANLESS

CARA WILLIAMS

PENDIUM
PUBLISHING HOUSE
514-201 Daniels Street
Raleigh, NC 27605

For information, please visit our Web site at
www.pendiumpublishing.com

PENDIUM Publishing and its logo are registered trademarks.

Six Years Manless
Copyright © 2008 by Cara Williams

Printed in the United States of America
ISBN: 978-0-9816883-4-3

PUBLISHER'S NOTE
Unless otherwise identified, Names, characters, places and incidents either are the product of the author's imagination or have been changed to protect the welfare and privacy of the person(s), and any resemblance to actual persons, living or dead, business establishments, events, or locales is entirely coincidental.

Without limiting the rights under the copyright reserved above, no part of this publication may be reproduced, stored in or introduced into a retrieval system, or transmitted , in any form, or by any means (electronic, mechanical, photocopying, recording, or otherwise), without the prior written permission of both the copyright owner and the above publisher of this book.

If you purchased this book without a cover you should be aware that the book is stolen property. It was reported as "unsold and d estroyed" to the publisher and neither the author nor the publisher has received any payment for this "stripped book."

This book is printed on acid-free paper.

Table of Contents

In Memory of My Mother

Due to the will of my Jehovah, who provided me with the ability to write, and my mother who always inspired me at a young age to write, but it was too late for her to read any of my book. However, I have written my first book. If it had not been for my mother and the help of my family, I would have not been able to express myself to write.

SIX YEARS
MANLESS

CHAPTER ONE

Today is Kara Baker's big day. It is her birthday. She's another year older, and oh boy how time just flies right on by you! Hell, one day you're a young lady, the next day you're a mother, and then the next day you're a good, old, grey-headed grandmother.

She was smiling to herself. Kara had been taking care of her family most of her life. First, her sister and brother, and now her own family. But today she is all alone, no one to care for anymore. Kara was studying her reflections in the mirror. There were a few lines around her mouth, her eyes, and forehead. Yes, Ms. Gray is looking for a long time home to lay around in, she and her whole family in her dark, brown hair. So Kara knows that it's about that time to start looking at life in a different way. She is sliding right into middle age. Yes, it is that time to start some of that quality time. She needs to start treating herself to some luxury, a little excitement, and some fun, too. Boy, she sure needs it, too. She has earned that quality time. Kara does not look her age. She looks much younger. She is a healthy and happy woman all the time. So what more could she be asking for except to try to live it to the best of her abilities. She has spent most of her life being a mother to two most marvelous boys and her two beautiful nieces, and she has raised four wonderful children. In between that time, she operated her own travel agency. So Kara thought it was time to take herself on a fantastic cruise. She really needed a vacation. She is always booking trips for other people. So now it is her time to be the other party to take a trip somewhere besides home all the time. Now she is going to have a life of her own after all.

Ms. Kara is going to take a cruise to the islands. Now there's more to this trip. It is a birthday gift to herself. Take a good look at this picture. One day my girl is all alone, and, for six years she has been without a man in her life at all. Now, three months later, here comes Mr. Right riding in on a big, white horse and swept my girl right off her feet. Now she is taking a two week vacation with a complete stranger. This is the first time she has ever received a gift that big before, not even once from that husband of hers. Now you tell me. What more could a woman ask for than to try and live it to the highest? She will be taking the first two weeks in March.

Now let's look at another picture of her. Kara is getting ready to take her trip with this man and hasn't told her family about neither the man nor the trip. The only people who know about this trip are her best friends, Dr. and Mrs. Helen Nicholas. They are the ones who introduced her to the man in the first place.

Kara has never, ever had a vacation with her children, and now she is taking one with Larry Grant. It's 8 a.m., and no one has called to wish her a happy birthday yet. Her family knows she is a very early riser. She is thinking to herself about all the things she and her kids used to do together, and she begins to smile. How time just flies right on by you. It was like yesterday. They were children, and now they're all grown up into young adults.

Well, it is getting to be that time to go do some shopping for this trip. She needs some new clothes, and, anyway, it has been a very long time since she has brought any clothes for herself. Kara walks down the hall and picks up her car keys on the table. She is ready to do a little shopping for today. She walks out of the house, gets into the car, and is on her way to the mall. Kara did not like to be in large crowds. She likes to shop very early in the morning. Her thoughts were the early bird always gets the worm. There are not a lot of people, just a few people at the mall when she arrives.

Kara arrives at the mall and found a good parking space. Once inside the mall, she starts looking into a few store windows. Kara has her own favorite store where she does all her shopping, and it's Pam Brown's shop, her best friend, She walks into Pam's place, and a young salesgirl helps here with finding all the clothes that she needs. She has everything from nighties to matching loungewear, evening gowns, three-piece pantsuits, and formal suits. The sales assistant also helps her with some casual clothes and shoes. Kara is now all set for her cruise.

Pam, the store owner, is five feet six inches in height and weighs 105 pounds. She is light-complexion with long, sandy hair and large green eyes. She is a beautiful but childless woman. Pam is also the perfect godmother to Kara and Helen's children. She doesn't play around when it comes down to her babies. She will raise hell about them to the mother and father.

"Well, well, Ms. Thang. Today is your birthday. So I'm wishing you a happy one. This is your gift from me and Ronald. And,

Ms. Thing, are you happy with everything? Did you get all you need?"
"Yes, Pam,"
"Well now, Ms. Thing, what's this? You're buying new clothes.
It looks like you're getting a brand new wardrobe. Come on now. You
know you don't spend any money on yourself unless it's a special
occasion. Now, my girl is not getting married because I would know all
about it. So let's have it.
"Well, Pam, I'm taking a trip. So I thought I would by me
some clothes for this occasion."
"Oh!
"You know that I'm very happy. I don't have a thing to
complain about. You know this is my favorite store, and I do all my
shopping here because you have everything that I need except groceries.
Oh, come on! You know that you are my best and dearest friend!"
"Yeah, right!" said Pam. "So, Miss Thing, you're finally going
to take that vacation. In all this time, you have never taken a day off of
your job unless it had something to do with your children. So, now,
Ms. Thing, you need to start talking to me, and I mean right now!"
"Well Pam, it's like this. I met this man, and we have been
talking about a two week vacation. I was going to tell you all about it."
"Oh, hell no! You just wait one minute! You can't be telling
me there's a man is in your life."
"Yes, Pam, but ..."
"But what, Miss Thang? A man just walked into your life. So
we're off to who knows where?"
"Pam, I'm taking a two week trip to Bermuda with him. It's a
gift from him."
Well, well Miss Thang, a new man just up and walked into your
life, and you're off to some island for two whole weeks with this 'Mr.
Man.' One thing I would like to know is whether or not my kids know
about this man and trip?"
"Well, no, Pam."
"Oh hell, Kara Baker, you can't be telling me the children
haven't ever met the man and doesn't know about the trip. Hell girl!
You're falling on your job! You can't be telling me you haven't said a
thing to my children about this man and a cruise!"
"Well, you get it, Pam."
"Okay, Miss Thang. A new man walks into your life, and
you're off to the islands for two weeks with Mr. Right. So, when will
we get a chance to meet this man before you go running off to some
Bermuda with this strange man, my dear friend? Are your kids going to
meet this man?"

"Yes, my family will meet the man and my mother, Mrs. Pam."

"Yeah, right, Miss Thang. How did you meet this man in the first place?

"My God, Pam! Helen and Willie introduced me to the man. He is Willie's best friend. They brought him over for me to meet. He is a very dear friend of the Nicholas' family."

"What is the man's name?"

"His name is Larry Grant. Now come on, Pam! You will get a chance to meet him. That's a big promise. Look, I am long overdue. I must be leaving now. Your customers will be coming in soon. Remember you are open for business."

"Ha, ha to you, Ms. Thang! Are you trying to tell me to mind my business? Oh no! Baby girl, you know better than that. I will be talking to you later on tonight. We will continue the conversation, okay! Now I must dismiss myself. I do love talking to you, but time is flying right on by. Good day, love, kiss-kiss."

"Come and give me a big hug and kiss, and do thank my brother, Ronald, for my birthday gift and lots of kisses and hugs.

"Good day, love, and the same to you."

Kara walks out of the store and proceeds to her car. She climbs into the car and heads toward home. The traffic is already jammed on the freeways. She had to stop at the grocery store. She needs to do some shopping in order to prepare dinner for the evening. She needs a few special items to go along with the chocolate cake that she is planning to bake for her granddaughter. She loves her grandchildren.

Kara returns home. It was still on the early side of the morning, but at least all of her shopping was completed. She still has awhile before the family comes over. After storing all the groceries away, she walks down the hallway, and the phone begins to ring. She walks over to the phone and answers it. Her oldest sister was on the other end wishing her a happy birthday. They talked for awhile, and then she brings the conversation to an end by saying everyone sends their love to her. Kara is now getting a little hungry. She decides to make herself a chicken salad sandwich with a cup of French Vanilla coffee. She always has a cup of coffee first thing in the morning. Unfortunately, this morning things were changed around a little. Shopping came first this morning. So Kara decided to sit, relax, and have a snack. After finishing her snack, she begins making the cake and then decided to get dinner ready. The family will be coming over for her big day, and she has always been the one to cook for the family.

Just then the doorbell rings. She wasn't expecting anyone this early in the day. She began to wonder who could it be coming by this early in the day. It was too early for the kids. Well, one thing about it. She will never know if she doesn't go to the door to see.

Kara goes to the front door and opens it. To her surprise, on the other side of the door is a big smile. It was the other best friend. In her hands were a large box and two large bags.

"Happy Birthday and good morning! How does it feel to be another year older, old, girl?" she said laughing at Kara.

"Well, Good morning to you, too, and do come in," Kara said.

Kara begins to pick up one of the bags and walks behind her friend into the kitchen.

"Hey, what are you cooking that smells so good? You can't be cooking for the Baker tribe again."

"You know it," says Kara.

Helen Nicholas is a very beautiful woman with honey-nut complexion. Her hair is light brown, and her eyes are light grey. She is six feet and two inches tall and weighs 110 pounds.

Kara, Helen, and Pam have been the best of friends all through school. They all grew up together. They had gone through some good times and bad times but had never stopped being the best of friends.

Helen is dressed in a white, three-piece pantsuit. She is looking good in it! Her hair was hanging loose down her back. Helen always looks cool all the time. She is a college professor, and her husband is a medical doctor. He specializes in women.

The three girls are the best of friends. They entered kindergarten together and continued their education journey all the way through high school and graduated. Upon completion of graduation, they all had their wedding. It was a triple one for the three 'Jersey Girls.' Pam Brown married a bank president. She and her husband have no children. Helen and her husband have two children, a boy and a girl. Kara Baker married a big-time building constructor and a woman lover. She was the first one to get a divorce. Pam opened a clothing store. Helen is the college professor, and Kara owns her own travel agency. So the 'Jersey Girls' have good lives. Helen went back to the door to get the other bag and returned to the kitchen. Kara and Helen put the bags on the table. Helen tells Kara that she and Willie went to the Farmer's Market this morning.

"I thought you might would appreciate some fresh fruits and vegetables. They were on sale today, so, old, dear friend, I decided to look out for you this morning."

Kara was smiling, "That was so sweet of you and Willie to do that for just little, old me. That was very thoughtful of you two."

"Yeah right! Do you want to pick out what you want?"

"Oh yes," says Kara.

Kara starts working in silence, putting away the fruits and vegetables. Helen asks Kara again what was smelling so good.

"Like I said, you're cooking for that Baker Tribe. Are they all coming over today?"

"Yes, you're right. My tribe will be coming by today."

Helen turns to her.

"Alright, old girl, this is your day. So open your presents. It is from the whole Nicholas Tribe with lots of love and kisses. Now my friend, we do have some talking to do. That is the reason I took my better half home so I could talk to you, and he wouldn't be in my way."

"Yes, right. You don't want him to tell you to mind your business."

The two started to laugh.

"Hey, some girl talk -- a few questions. Now Kara, you know that Dr. and I will always have your back. We would never misjudge you about anything. We love you too much for that. We have always been at your side at all times."

"Oh, Helen, you are the best. I do hope you will be by my side because if I so much as fall, I will need someone to pick me up, someone that understands. Helen, would you like to talk about your friend and mine?"

"Yes," says Helen.

"Oh sis', well I do have some kind of relationship with Mr. Larry Grant. We have developed slowly over the past six months. We have occasionally dated and had a few kisses, but hell, Helen, I'm still one of the small fishes in a tiny pool."

She was looking at Kara.

"Oh, come on sweet. I strongly advise you to take this trip with Larry. You need a life! So little Sis'', go for it, okay? My man is crazy about you.

"Yeah, right. And thanks a lot. Your girl just jumped all over me about this man and really tripping this morning. She asked me some questions about him. She wants to meet him, and she is mad as hell with me because I didn't tell her and the kids about him. Helen you know how she is when it comes down to her godchildren. She loves them. She is mother number two."

"Yes, you're right Kara. You know how Pam is. She is very funny when it comes down to all the children. You also know that we never keep anything away from one or the other since day one. Come on Kara, we always tell each other everything. We've never kept secrets from one another. We have always been loyal to each other."

"Hell, Pam is the same way with my kids. You know how she is. Anyway, you and Dr. Willie started this entire mess in the first place. You two had to bring this man over, talking about I like you to meet our best friend. So I met Mr. Right like a good friend would do. Now I've kept things away from my best friend and my children. I did tell her she would be seeing him very soon. I've also decided to tell the kids today, and that's my promise."

Helen was smiling at Kara.

"Well, well it's about time," says Helen.

She crosses her arms over her chest. She sits down at the table and looks at Kara.

"Okay old girl, don't start that worrying all over again, okay? You still have some time but not too much. Listen to me. Take my advice. Sit your family down and tell them all about Larry and your vacation all in one big nutshell."

Kara smiles at Helen.

"Come on, sis', you know that number one son can be a little bull-headed and a bit stubborn, too."

"I will talk to the children. Kara will start to cry if you look at her the wrong way."

Now the teardrops begin to well-up in her eyes. Kara is beginning to open her gifts. She is surprised to see the most beautiful, sexy dress. She begins to laugh and cry at the same time and gave Helen a hug and kiss.

"Thank you and the entire Nicholas family for me, and please kiss and hug everyone of them for me. I love you! Helen, you and Pam are the best. Pam and Ronald gave me a new look. Today they purchased all of my new clothes. I will forever be grateful for having the two of you in my life. I love you with all my heart."

Kara and Helen both at this moment begin to cry.

"You're the best."

"Yes, we know," said Helen.

"You're right, you know. I haven't had a man in six long years. Hell, I have been an ice-cold woman all this time. In this dress you gave me, I will become a hot, sexy mother."

Kara and Helen were crying and laughing again.

"Helen, you know what? We need Pam here with us now. It would be like in the olden days."

"You're right, crying and laughing. Yes, that was the good old days. So much fun to remember. Boy! We would talk all night about marriage and wedding bells and who would have the biggest diamond."

Ms. Helen was the first one to get the sexy man at school, the big diamond ring, and the big man. She starts laughing.

"Alright, you just leave my adorable husband alone."

"Yes, but you and Pam were the first to get the sexy men. Mine was the sexiest. The women were running after him. Then he just started to run with the wolves."

"I will call Pam before the day is over with. You know, Helen, sometimes I have this terrible feeling that life is just rushing right on by me like I'm just standing still, like I'm standing in a time zone."

"Now come on Kara, didn't you say you wished Larry would treat you less like mother superior and more like an earth woman."

She was laughing.

"Well yes, but...oh, no, no, believe me. This little dress will light a fire so hot that no man could resist putting his hands in the red hot flames. Boy, he will be smiling from ear-to-ear with a big smile on his face that you won't be able to take away."

"Helen, you're bad but a damn good friend all the way to old girl," says Kara.

"Yes, I know," says Helen. "But I would like very much for you to stop worrying about everybody and start enjoying your life for once. So will you please do that for yourself and me?"

"Helen, I doubt if my life will ever be quite the same again. I simply didn't believe that in all this time I would actually find a man. My God, Helen, I was never looking for one either. I've been manless for six years and up comes one now. I call myself courting or dating again. Now that's one big laugh to me."

"Well, yes," said Helen. "That's one big one alright, but it is about time you start to live again. You are always worrying about everyone but never thinking about no one. Kara, I see you as being so devoted to your family and your business until you can't see anything that is for you. Hell, you're talking about you're still some little fish in a small pond. Well, young lady, you are going to be a big ass fish in a big pond (ocean), and a big ass shark is moving right beside you with some quick movements. And you're not going to be able to shake him, can you, Ms. Thang?"

She gave Kara a second hug.

"Now sweetness, don't you start that worrying all over again. You still have some time left but not too much is there? Now you take care of your personal, Kara. I don't want to see you all dried up before your time. My God, we've been through a lot together, some bad times and some good times, too. We all went through a crying time with your separation and with the divorce, but we're still here, the four of us. We are the reliable ones Kara."

"I am very aware of the four, Boss!"

"Okay Ms. Thang," says Helen. "Larry has already paid for this trip. So Kara, you need a life. Little sis,' I think I have talked out."

"Yeah, you're right. I do need to get a life. I know you and Pam are right, but I haven't had a man in my life since lover boy Mike walked out on me six years ago. My God, Helen, not one man has ever asked me out on a date, let alone to dinner or a movie. Hell, I was always looking down on men. I realized I didn't have much confidence or trust in any men. Mr. Mike took all that away with him. So I put myself in safe mode away from all the other wolves. Now I'm going out with one of the wolves. You know something, Helen? To be perfectly honest with you, I didn't want to meet this man. I never told you this, but one day your husband came by my job and told me if I didn't meet this man I was going to be by myself spending the remainder of my life all alone. Even my grandchildren will be all gone away and never ever look back at me. I will be here sitting all by myself looking, hoping every day that Mike might decide to come back. He said if he hasn't returned in six years, then it was time for me to get up off my ass and start to smell the damn coffee for a change because you four were moving the hell on. He said he was talking to me as a big brother and not as a friend. Helen, Dr. Willie shook up my happy little home without a giggle or a laugh. I was crying like hell. He looked at me and said no more. He then walked out of the door and didn't look back."

"Oh my! Did Doc say all that to you?"

"Yes, he did."

"Kara, he never said a word to me about having this talk with you. I know the first time I mentioned Larry to you, you told me, no."

"Yes, I did, but Mr. Boss changed that song for me."

She was laughing, not crying this time.

"Helen, I needed that talk because you and Pam are always holding my hand, but not Mr. Doc. He talked to me as if he was talking to one of his patients. My God, Helen, I deserved that. All I was doing was destroying my life and everyone that came along."

"Kara, I'm so glad that Willie talked to you because we love you. Mike has never been the best when it came right down to you. One thing about Mike. He is a good father to his children. He would give them everything they would ask for. Now the grandchildren, those are his heart, but the man is not a good husband. Willie and Ronald were always at your ex-husband's neck. One night my Willie was so mad with Mike that he told him that he would operate on him like he does surgery on his female patients. Kara in all the years I have been married to Willie, I have never seen him that angry. He would always walk away, but this time my man was about to cut up your ex-husband. Pam and Ronald kept talking to him. I asked Mike to please leave. Pam told us not to tell you anything about that night."

"Oh my God, Helen, now you tell me about this incident."

"Oh hell, Kara, you were so much in love with Mike you would have disagreed with everything anybody told you about that man. We say right, and you say wrong. So to keep you happy, we just kept it to ourselves and waited for today."

"Mike said you people were bad influences on me. That you people were crazy as hell. I just looked at the man. Now I know why you people are so crazy."

She started to laugh.

So bro' Willie was going to cut up my husband and turn him into a female."

Helen and Kara started to laugh.

"Well Kara, it's about time for me to head home to my family. I'm sure they are expecting me any moment now. Oh, are you going out tonight to celebrate your birthday with Mr. Grant?"

"Yes."

"Well, my friend, do not call me when you get home tonight. Oh, Kara, don't look so down-hearted. Larry is good for you. Please believe me. If he wasn't, I wouldn't have introduced you to him. Kara you are so devoted to your family and your job. Please start to live a little for all of us, okay Kara?"

"Yes, Mom Helen. But, my God, Pam makes me look like I'm not a very good mom or a very good friend after that outburst today."

"Kara, our Pam will be alright. She is angry with you right now, but before the day is over with she will be her old self again. So you make sure you call her later today or tonight."

"Okay, Mom Dearie. I will, but I was wrong and very much unjust. I made a big mistake by not telling her or the kids about this trip and Larry."

"My Kara, you are right one way and wrong another way. I'm on your side. You need to start reliving your life again. Also, start to think about yourself for once. If not, you will fall right back into that dark hole that was holding you for years. Kara, I don't want you to become all dried up before your time. My God, Kara, we all have been with you through a lot of bad times and good times when your marriage just fell apart. Pam and I were right by your side. We are still there for you, your two good old reliable friends, one for all. Kara, we are not complaining. We all just love you and would like for you to have a good life again. You have met a good, hardworking man that likes you for yourself."

"Helen, I know that you would never complain. You and Pam are the best. I'm the luckiest person in the world to have such good friends. Yes, the three 'Jersey Girls.'

"No more secrets. Always the truth to one another, okay? Now I must be leaving right now. If not Doc will be calling me, asking what's the hold up? So I think I need to be walking out the door right about now. Kara you and Mr. Larry have a good time tonight, okay?"

Kara was walking with Helen to the door. She stops at the door, hugs Kara, and tells her she loves her and to enjoy the remainder of the morning. Kara says the same to back.

"Love you and give all my love to the family."

Helen walks to her car and drove away. Kara closes the door and walks back down the hallway to her room. She is thinking about calling Brian's office to talk to him, but she decides to wait a little longer before she calls him. She thinks about Larry and smiles. She walks into her bedroom to put away her gift that Helen had brought to her. My God, this is one sexy, red dress. The most beautiful, sexiest dress she had ever seen in her life. If she should wear this hot number Larry just – oh. Kara stopped thinking to herself. Kara went back into the kitchen to make herself a pot of coffee. She is about to call Pam when the front door opened. In walked her entire family. Well, there's no need to call Brian now. He was at the house, and the whole Baker tribe was on hand. She is all smiles. Her loving family is all at the house at one time, and she is so happy. Her three daughters, two sons and her two grand-children. She can stop all the worrying now. The whole tribe is there. Her two boys – Brian, the oldest, was married and had two children. Mary is his wife and Michelle and Mark are his kids. John, her other son, has no wife but lots of women. He is like his father in every way. Her two nieces, Diane, the oldest, and Carol. Now Carol is Pam's heart. You can't say anything about Miss Carol because if you do you will get into a lot of trouble with Pam, and you got something on your hands. Don't get me wrong. Pam loves all the children, but she says Carol is her daughter and also Helen's daughter, Crystal. She thinks the two young ladies are the Miss University.

CHAPTER TWO

Brian walks into the room, hugs and kisses his mother, and says, "Well Happy Birthday Mom. We are all her for your big day.

"Hi Nana! We all have a big gift for you and some flowers, too. Can I have my hug and kiss? You my Nana. I love you so much says," Michelle.

"Oh yes, my little Nell, I love you too with lots of kisses and hugs."

Mark says, "Hi Nana, we are all so hungry and happy birthday to you. I love you."

"Okay, Mr. Mark, I love you, too, and you can get ready to eat. Okay, my Mark?"

He just laughed and said, "Oh Nana, I'm no Mr. Mark."

All the others wished her a happy birthday. Kara was so happy she was hugging and kissing all her children and crying a little. She was so glad that the whole family came over at one time for a pleasant change.

Nell says, "Oh my Nana, guess what? We didn't go to work today. We all took the day off for your special day.

"Okay, Nell, you talk too much," says Mark.

"That's okay, Mark," says Mary. "Mom, here are some flowers. We all love you."

She hugs Kara and gave her large bouquet of red roses.

"My, they are so beautiful. I'll go and put them in some water." A little teardrop fell. She walked away.

"Come on girl let's put the food on the table. Everything is ready."

Kara and the girls went into the kitchen. She quickly dished up the food to be put on the dining room table. Kara has baked a pot roast, backed chicken, vegetables, rice, potato salad, a chocolate cake with mixed ice cream, and ice tea. She called everyone to come into the dining room to eat. Everyone is now sitting at the table. Diana blessed the table. The meal was pleasantly. Much to her relief the evening was beginning to wear to an end. She was thinking about how to tell her family about the trip and the man all in one big nutshell. Hell, those were Helen's words.

Then everyone returned for seconds to eat.

"I have a chocolate cake and ice cream and little Pearl, it's your favorite."

"Oh my Nana, thank you. Mother said this is your day. What does she mean? I thought everyday was your day."

"Oh my sweet Pearl, you know that today is my birthday. So that is why your mother said it is my day."

"Oh, right. That's why we are all here for your big day. That's why we took today off."

"Okay, little one, I love you all for this day."

Kara was thinking to herself. It was time to talk to the family.

"Well, my family, I need everyone to remain in your seat. I need to talk to everybody about some very important business. Whatever the circumstances are will be my injustices, and I will have to take. My little talk is well overdue, but it's just a little misunderstanding on my part. Well, my family, your mother is going to take a two-week vacation."

To her relief everyone was laughing and talking.

"Oh mother, that is so nice, you are going to take a vacation," says Diana.

"Yes, baby but I didn't finish telling you all other part of it. I'm sorry that it took me so long to tell you, but the time wasn't right. I'm taking a fantastic cruise. I need a break. The first two weeks of March is when I'm planning to go. It was a gift from a dear friend. My friend's name is Mr. Larry C. Grant. He will be my companion on the ship. He is a very close friend of mine. So children, let's not all speak at one time."

Ms. Carol was the first one to speak.

"Oh God! Mother you didn't say you would be taking a two week trip with a man. I just know you didn't say a man – not my mother. Oh, come on Ms. Thang you sure you're the woman who said a few years ago that all men were nothing but snakes in the grass. Oh no, you can't be telling me a thing about a man, not my dear, old mother."

"Oh stop it, Carol, and shut your mouth tight, that big mouth of yours. Close it before I close it for you," said Diana. "Mother, we all are very happy for you. Now this is a very special day for you. She gave her mom a hug and a kiss. Now tell us what's so special about this vacation and man."

"Mary, would you just look at mom? She is blushing."

"A vacation and stepping out with a man on her arms. You go Ms. Thang. My oh my, you're a bad little mom. I'm so glad you are finally getting a life," said Diana.

"What about your clothes?" asked Mary.

"I went to Aunt Pam's today and did some shopping earlier this morning. I have just about everything I need."

"How is Aunt Pam?"

"She is doing fine, just a little angry with me."

"Angry about what, Mom? She's angry about the trip and the man, but I will talk to her later on tonight."

"Nana, can I go with you on your vacation? I'll be a good girl."

"Little Pearl, you can't go with Nana this time, okay?"

"Well Nana, let's open the gift I brought you."

Nell took the box and opened it. Upon opening the box, out came a pretty three piece black and white pant suit.

"Kids, I love this pants suit. Now I have two new gifts that are very beautiful."

"Mother, will you please stop crying. Let's take a look at the other clothes since you've found a man. You need to be looking good at all times. I can't believe my mother finally found herself a man. Well, well, it's about time you found yourself a man. I hope this means you are going to start living your life again, because you know he will never come back home to live again that's for sure."

"Mom's been holding out on us. Ms. Thang has stepped out on the world. Well, go on with your bad self," said John. "So you got life back in order. You do know that you are not obligated to anyone except yourself. Your little off springs are all grown-up. So you go for it, old girl, with your sexy self! You're right. You are well overdue. Old Pop has suddenly been pushed over by a rich man."

"John, what are you talking about?" said Kara, and all the others in the family.

"Mother, you did say you were taking this trip with a man named Larry Grant. Old girl you have found yourself a wealthy man. You know, mother, the man can buy you an island and still have a small gold mine. Like I always said, Uncle Willie doesn't socialize with any poor class people. Only the classiest first rate ones."

"Mother, you really don't know who Larry Grant is, do you? His father is the president of all the largest hotel chains around the world. Mother, he has walked in and taken over the number one hotels downtown. He is an all business man. He will step right over the little man."

"John, I need you to stop talking for one minute. I didn't say how I met the man."

"How did you meet this man? I know that your Uncle Willie knows about Larry."

"Well, old lady, you know my uncle keeps me up to date. So I knew Uncle Willie and Aunt Helen were coming by with him, Mr. Grant."

"John, you didn't say one word to me about this man the other week. You asked me was I ready to talk, and I said talk about what? John you just looked at me and smiled and said, "Well, okay old lady,– and you knew all the time." John tell me one thing, have you met Larry?"

"Yes mother, we talked, he and Uncle Willie play golf together every Wednesday, and I go along with them. The day you got your visit from Uncle Willie, and Aunt Helen was talking about him, you said you didn't want to meet him. Uncle Willie got into his car, drove off, and never said a word. We stayed at the club and had a few drinks."

"You would keep everything to yourself," said Kara.

"Now Mom, I love you. And I love you, too, John."

"Carol, well here goes Mr. Brian with his mouth wide open. The man is going to have court. Today our own mother is on trial, and we are the jury. Mary, you're the judge. Okay, Brian, has the floor. He may just put John on trial since he knows so much."

She was laughing.

"Yes. Right, Carol you have all the funnies. Anytime you want, Carol, you can object to me when you disagree with me, but come on you two. Please stop the injustice with one another," said Kara. "You go ahead and complain if it makes you feel better."

"Okay mother. Seriously, we need to meet this Mr. Grant before you go running off with this man on a trip. You know we don't know anything about him. And mother you will be too far from home with a complete strange man."

"Brian, come on," said John. "I know the man. Okay, Brian my foot is down on this one, this is our own mother we're talking about and not some hoochie woman."

"See, I told you the lawyer had the floor. A hoochie woman. Mother, you say that Aunt Helen and Uncle Willie are very good friends of this man, right? Here come the judges, Mary and Carol. Let it go," said Diana. "Miss Goody-two-shoes is on the floor now. Alright Carol, that is enough."

"Yes, mom."

"Alright everybody, just keep your head on. I will ask Larry to come over Sunday for a late dinner so that all of you will get a chance to meet him. I will call all of you and give you a time to be here," said Kara.

"Look mother, I want to know what he has in mind about you. I will not accept him coming in half-stepping, ever. You are not some hoochie woman, and I'm just keeping it real. Mother, I do think we deserve some answers. Don't forget you are the only mother we have, and no one else can fulfill your place."

"My sweet Brian. Thank you my sons and daughters. I love you all."

Brian asked his mother exactly how long was it going to be before you were going to tell us about Mr. Grant.

"This vacation break, you did say in two weeks right?"

"Now look here son. What I do with my private life is my own business. So please don't go getting it all wrong. I do love that you care for me and worry about me. But son, I do need to live my life a little, too. You know it has always been the children and me. So like I said, this is your mother's time."

"Mother, you are so right, so do close your mouth, Brian, and let's go home. We will all see you Sunday, mother," said Mary.

"Well the judge has closed the court room," said Carol.

Kara had to laugh at Carol herself this time. The whole Baker tribe has come, and now they are ready to depart.

"Mother," Diana says, "Baby, you do know that daddy didn't like Uncle Willie. Now he's going to really hate him now that you have a new man in your life. So, mother, I wish you all the best with this relationship."

The whole family said good night. She walked the children to the door and hugged everyone and said good-bye. Kara wasn't going to allow this evening to upset her tonight. She always had known that her son was a hard case to crack. He is so much like his father. Well, she needs to start getting her own life together if only for tonight. She was going to try and look her best. She walked into her bedroom, started stripping off her clothes, and stood naked in front of the mirror. She looked at her body, she had a light dark-chocolate complexion with dark, brown hair and light brown eyes. She was five feet two inches tall. She has a nice, slender figure. She went into the bathroom to take a bubble bath with soft crystals. Kara was smelling the perfume that reminded her of her ex. He liked that softened powder. She was thinking about Mike. He just up and walked out on her. Boy, Mike was a big, black sexual animal-looking man. And I just had to taste the damn, dark-black chocolate. But Hell, ten years down the long, rocky road, all the chocolate and black suddenly disappeared, and all the sex was just immune. No feelings, oh well. No fire on the heater was left behind. Everything had worn off. She was giggling to herself. Damn he was a very unfaithful man. Just a big, black, old snake that crawls from one hole to another. He's the best when it comes to his children. He is absolutely an adorable father to his children. Well, one out of two isn't bad. She was smiling. She had to stop and think and start getting ready. Larry was coming to pick her up at seven o'clock. She needs to be ready because Mr. Larry does not like to wait on anyone. I think I will wear something on the sexy side.

Kara was sitting in front of the mirror applying a little make-up on. She slipped her arm into a cool, sexy, black satin dress that wrapped around her body. She has a slender body with curves everywhere they should be. She was completed. She stared at her reflections in the long footed mirror and gave a nod of satisfaction. She was looking good and beautiful. Larry was taking her out to dinner. She was to dine at one of the best restaurants. He had chosen candle light and some soft light music.

Kara was ready and waiting when Larry came. He was to call at seven thirty. Boy, he was right on time. It was exactly seven thirty. The doorbell rang. She went to the door.

"Hello Larry, Yes, back to you."

He walked into the living room. She saw the swift look of approval in Larry's eyes. Kara eyed him uncertainly.

"Do I take it that you approve."

"Wasn't I suppose to?" he laughed huskily.

"I really do take your opinion into account."

Kara was looking at this tall, good-looking, muscular man with jet black hair, light brown eyes, and light brown complexion with the most beautiful white teeth. He has on a black dinner suit with a snow white shirt and a black, velvet tie.

"You look good enough to draw a room full of women waiting to jump your bones."

"I have to look the part," he said. "But, sexy momma, I'm all yours tonight."

"Yeah, right," echoed Kara.

Larry and Kara begin walking out to his Porsche. As he placed a hand on her arm to help her into the car, he then settled himself into the seat beside her. Edging out of the driveway into traffic.

"Larry."

"Yes," he replied.

"Where exactly are we going?" she asked.

"Somewhere the food is very good, and the waiters can't hover over you. And of course, no loud music. It's also Greek food. It is owned by my friend. He's Greek. Do you like Greek food?"

"I've never actually had any Greek food before, but I will try some."

"Well, in that case it will be another new experience. I'm sure you will enjoy it."

Kara turned to stare out of the window trying to shake off the nervous feeling. Larry was far too sure of what would please her. The car drove up outside the restaurant. Larry was opening her door and escorting her into the restaurant. Upon their arrival, they were greeted by the owner.

"Hello my old friend. It is so good to see you again. Where have you been for so long? We have missed you so much."

"You know how it is at times, Leo. Always business."

"Yeah, but a man must still eat."

"You're right, Leo."

He was laughing. Kara was watching the two men as they exchanged greetings before they were led to a table. There were fresh flowers on the table and a candle flickering. It was so romantic. This brought back a sudden and unexpected tightness to her throat. Larry was look at her.

"Kara, is something wrong with you?"

"Oh no!" she replied, sitting quickly in the chair Leo was holding for her. "This just fine," she smiled at Larry.

Leo returned with the menus. Kara was focusing her attention deliberately on the menu. Her expressions were changing. The menu was quite confusing to her.

She looked at Larry saying, "I'm sorry. I know everything is translated into English, but I have no idea what to choose."

"Okay, baby, then I'm afraid for once you'll have to trust me, or is that asking too much?"

She threw him a quality look.

"Okay, Mr. Larry on the subject of food. I'm prepared to accept your judgment. After all, you're the expert. Plus, I'm not too difficult to please."

His brown eyes darkened. Pools of dark brown.

"Kara, I say you are powerful. You do know I'm a little cautious perhaps, but when you find the courage I'm sure the results will be far more rewarding than you could ever have imagined," he said.

Kara was blushing. She realized he had deliberately given a

double edge to the words.

"Larry, I'm talking about the food."

"Yes, of course baby! What else?"

He gave their order to Leo. The two men started talking and laughing together. Kara was watching them. It struck her that he was completely at ease with her. He seemed to be laughing more with Leo than he did with her. Both men turned around and looked at her. She guessed she had become the subject of their conversation. She smiled, but she was so nervous. She waited until Leo had taken their order and left before saying anything.

"Larry, were you and Leo talking about little, old me? I'm very cautious or perhaps, being a little on the nosey side."

"Well, my little nosey, sweet Kara, I was asking him about his family, so don't you get offended," he said quickly. "The Greeks like to ask lots of questions. And when they know all about you, you become a dear friend for life."

The food arrived.

"This looks good. What is it?"

"I think you are going to like it. It has a very delicate flavor. It is pork kebabs."

"Larry, I'm very cautious about most foods that I eat. I don't usually try something new until I find out about its safety."

"Nothing is that safe, Kara. Sooner or later you have to come out and face the world. Look baby, you can't spend your hold life behind locked doors."

"Oh you're right, Mr. Grant. I was locked up for six years trying to make up my mind whether or not I still wanted to get involved with you snakes again. So you can just walk out of my life."

He was breathing very angrily.

"I don't play games, Kara. It's far, far too damn dangerous. Look baby, I'm nobody's snake. I didn't know I was playing a game. There are limits to the amount of restraint I possess. Hell girl, I want you."

That statement was simple for him. Oh my God, that's enough. She feels her heart beating very fast as their eyes meet across the table. She was trying so hard to look away but couldn't. The jet dark eyes were holding her and refused to let go. She had never felt this way before. She was getting some feelings that haven't been there before.

"Larry, it was a lovely meal."

Leo returned back to the table. Larry was saying something in Greek to him. They were ready to leave the restaurant. He paid the bill and said goodnight to Leo. He put his hand under her arm as he escorted her to the car.

She said, "Larry I have something to ask you," after he had closed the door behind her.

Going around to the driver's side of the car, he didn't look at her as he eased the Porsche back into the traffic.

She opened the window to let the breeze cool her cheeks, but it didn't do anything to lessen the tension which seem to crackle between them. It was a relief when they drove up outside her house. He walked her to the door. He took the keys from her nervous hand and unlocked the door, but he made no attempt to leave.

"Well, are you going to invite me in? You did say you had something to ask me. Also, it is custom to ask a date in for one last drink before the evening ends."

"Well, it's not my custom for one split second, but you're right I do need to talk to you about something."

She walked into the house. Larry was right behind her. He closed the door.

CHAPTER THREE

He turned around and took her in his arms. The steel-hard tension of his body as he drew her against him, his mouth seeking hers,

"Don't you run away from me, Kara," he said before his lips claimed hers.

"Kara, do you know the affect you have on me?"

Kara's heart was beating so loudly that she was certain he must have heard it. She was so shocked by what was happening. She had lived with a kind of sexual numbness, believing herself immune to the sort of emotions and desires he was forcing her to face. She had never ever been tempted to test. Simply because without feelings, there was no pain and no gain. That was the way she preferred it. She had been managing to fool herself until right now.

"Larry, can I offer you some coffee or some wine."

"Look here, Kara. I don't need any wine or coffee. All I want is to taste the strong sweetest of your soft lips and you body. I intend for both of us to be stone-cold sober when I come to you."

He came slowly towards her as if a little angry curse had taken possession. He kissed her mouth in a brutal kiss.

"Larry, we do need to talk about something."

She was trying to force her body to remain strong. She was trying very hard not to get weak.

"Kara, I need you, but like you said let's talk. I can wait. I have two weeks with you. So you can stop trying to run away. Like I said, I can wait. I don't give up that easily. You have to come out and stop fighting."

"Larry, I'm honestly looking forward to it. I just found out you had met my son, John. He didn't tell me. Larry, you are invited to the house Sunday to meet my family, the whole Baker family. I would like for them to meet you before you take me away," she smiled. "My son would like to check you out before you run away with his only mother for two whole weeks. So, Larry, would you please be so nice as to give me a time for Sunday?"

She was looking at him.

He smiled and said quietly, "Thank you for this opportunity to meet your family. So they are going to examine me good, right? You're right. I did meet John. He is alright in my book. He never said a thing about you. He was acting as if he didn't even know you. Willie was always talking about him and Helen. John just looked on. Until one day Willie got mad about something Helen said to him. He looked at John and said to him that mother of yours and that's how I found out he was your son. I had never met you. Yes, I would love to meet your other son. I'm quite capable of fighting my own battles, baby. I'm also giving you fair warning, Ms. Baker. I play by very different rules, and I certainly do not talk or take people prisoner when I know that sooner or later I will get just what I have always wanted."

He looked at Kara with a big laugh. Kara was shivering a little. There was something about this man that seemed to be a threat. Even though, she couldn't decide on precisely what the threat was. Larry Grant had the kind of look that would appeal to any woman, but right now she was of interest. She most definitely didn't like being threatened. Kara looking at Larry, "You don't know what you are saying." Larry was watching her face without any expressions.

"Oh, I know exactly what I'm saying, my little spring flower. I will be at your house around 4 p.m. And you make sure your sons are ready to meet me."

So the arrangements had been made. My God, I have been out of practice for a long time. Hell, six years is too long to start committing to someone.

"What's wrong Kara? I thought you were the young woman I met a couple of months ago. The lady who does as she pleases."

For the life of her, she couldn't think of anything to say. She didn't want him to think wrong things about her. Kara had cornered herself. Now she was embarrassed. He was laughing at her, and that made things even worse, but it was funny.

"Hey, come here. Look at me. I said look at me," he was smiling at her with a different sort of smile.

His eyes were gentle. He took her in his arms and held her gently. That had no sexuality about it this time.

"Little Flower, let's not part on bad terms. Listen to me for a moment. He held her away from him. He was looking down at her.

"Kara, you're a nice, young woman. I find you to be very delightful and attractive. I mean very attractive, but your ideas and your ways of looking at life are interesting. In many ways admirable, but they aren't realistic."

"Larry, I don't know what you mean."

"No, but if we continue to see one another, you will, my Little Spring Flower. Goodnight Kara."

He walked out the door.

She went to her room to get ready for bed. He was inevitable in her sleep. His words kept her awake that night. She had fallen in love with this man. There was no doubt about it. Now she was sunk. She turned over restlessly in bed, curling into a ball as if to protect herself.

"Yes, six years, no man, and now a man."

Her family had always been first. What will be next? Well, Kara has lost some sleep over Mr. Larry and her family.

The next morning she was up very early to have her French vanilla coffee. She picks up the phone to call Pam. She was supposed to call last night, but it was too late. She dials the phone. It is ringing. Pam's voice comes on the line.

"Good Morning!"

"Well, Ms. Thang, you decided to call me. Well, it's about time."

"Good morning to you, too, Pam. I didn't call last night because I didn't get home until late. But you're the first person I called this morning. Larry took me out for my birthday. The family wants to meet him and you. So I invited him to come over for dinner on Sunday. He said yes. So we will be having a late dinner at four o'clock p.m. You and Ronald are invited along with my family. My family should be here about four o'clock. Pam, I'm very sorry for keeping things away from you. This will never happen again."

She was smiling.

"Okay, Ms. Thang, we are still the Jersey Girls. I love you and, sure, I will bring something for Sunday's dinner."

"No, my love, just you and Ronald. And you have a good morning, love. I love you."

And good morning to you also Pam. She knows the next person to call is Helen and then her son. Kara picks up the receiver to call Helen. The phone was ringing. She answered it on the first ring.

"Well, good morning, Ms. Thang. You know it's about time you called me. I wanted to call last night, but Willie wouldn't let me call you. So, let's have it."

"Helen, good morning to you, too. Everything went along just fine. The whole tribe was over. The family took the news very well. But now, Helen, you know John already knows Larry. They had already met one another."

"Well, yes Kara. We will talk about that another day, okay?"

"Yes, if you say so. Anyway, Mr. Brian had more to say then anyone else. He wants to meet with Larry before we take this trip. So Sunday, he will get a chance to meet Mr. Grant. Carol and Brian are always ahead of the game. Larry will be coming over to meet with my family at four o'clock p.m. So, Sunday at four o'clock, I want you and Mr. Willie to come to the house for a late dinner. You know you two people were the ones that got me into this mess in the first place."

Helen was laughing at Kara.

"Helen, we went to a Greek restaurant. It was a nice place with candles light and soft music. The food was great. His friend, Leo, owns the restaurant. Oh yeah, everything was just smooth until my family came up. He was totally and completely up to par about the family, but he said he couldn't take any prisoners. He plays by his rules only. He was smiling when he said those words. Oh Helen, the man treats me like a queen."

"Kara, you'll be alright. You know we will be at your house Sunday. And girl, I will have your back!"

She was laughing so hard. You know I can't wait to tell Willie about this."

"Helen, he's tough alright. I think he eats bowls of nails every morning. Her voice was softening. I'm acting like a big fool. This man is sweating me hard. I can't think too good."

"Kara, you're a big girl now. Everything will start falling in place. Just let nature takes its course. Love you and good morning to you."

She hangs the phone up from talking to Helen. Now she was going in the kitchen to get a cup of coffee before she called her son. It was 8:30 a.m. It was time to make that call to Brian.

"Now here goes nothing."

The phone was ringing. On the second ring Brian answered.

"Hello mother, I was thinking about you."

"Good morning, my son. How is the family this morning?"

"All is just fine. mom. Mary and the kids are getting ready to go out this morning. So mother, did you talk to this man?"

"Oh! Yes, Mr. Lawyer man. I did talk to this man as you say, but his name is Mr. Larry Grant to you."

"Alright mom, but, mom, did you talk to him?"

"My God, son. Yes I did Lawyer son. Now you listen real good, my son, your mother is not absent-minded. Not yet anyway. Now son, you get off of your high horse and put your feet back on this ground. Your mother did talk to Mr. Grant. He will be meeting with the whole family on Sunday at 4 p.m. for a late dinner. Oh, by the way, did I say the whole family?"

"Yes, mom."

"Well, you aunts and uncles also will be coming. So I wanted to make sure your old mom didn't forget to tell you."

Kara was laughing at Brian.

"Mr. Lawyer man, you tell my other half? This is your little job to tell the others to be on time because I'm looking forward to this day. Mr. Brian will you be nice enough to kiss-kiss my babies for me and Mary, too. Good morning to you, my son. Your mother loves you."

She hung up the phone. Kara was not on a cloud today. She had an overcast morning. She felt this dark cloud close in over her. She has no self-esteem this morning, no sleep, and was being threatened by a man. All for one night. There were so many things that needed to be taken care of before this trip.

She needs a few days off of work. But that is a no-no. Today she will have to put two days into one. She will start with her house cleaning. Next, her shop. Now this is the time to use that good old housekeeper – right now. Hell, she was the maid the master all in one big package. Kara has to laugh at her own self this time. She's not complaining because she could really use some time for herself for a change. Her day was passing by very nicely. Kara went into the bathroom to take a shower. Maybe the bath would make her feel a little better. She walked into her bedroom to get dress so she could go and do some shopping. She also needs to stop at the ABC store. She needs some alcohol and some wine for her Sunday dinner. She was trying to figure out what to cook on Sunday in the first place. She has always loved cooking for a big crowd.

Kara put on a Jade colored pantsuit and a pair of copper colored sandals. She was all set to go and do her grocery shopping. She went and picked up the kind of items she would need for her special occasion. Well, it is her son's special occasion because he needs to meet the man. Everything was just fine the way it was before my son felt the need to become the prosecutor, the lawman, and the judge. My son has just put me on trial.

Kara has to laugh out loud again at herself. She was in front of her fireplace looking at the glowing red flames sipping at her coffee. She was actually thinking about last night with Larry. She was kind of feeling that her life was starting to come alive at last. The past year she had been a nice, cold woman but her brain seemed to have started to spring to life again. The last time she wanted to go to bed her brain went into working overtime. There were plenty of unanswered questions. It had reached the stage where she thought she knew the man or at least she thought she did but not really knowing the history of the man at all. Not his past nor present either. Come to think of it, she doesn't know one thing about Larry Grant.

"My God. I really haven't been looking at this package at all. Pam and Brian are right. I'm going to take a trip with a complete stranger for two whole weeks on a cruise ship. The man knows more about my life. Well, well, old girl, you did say you needed some excitement, lots of fun, and to keep yourself occupied at all times."

She was smiling.

Kara carried her empty cup into the kitchen where she washed and dried it and put it away. Suddenly, she felt exhausted and was shocked when she took a look at the clock to discover that it was well past midnight. Yet, she still felt too excited to go to bed until common sense kicked in and reminded her that she had to get up early and go to work in a few hours. And besides, she was leaving herself to feel trapped, yet strangely dissatisfied. She slipped off her robe and slid onto the bed naked between her silk sheets and closed her eyes, but sleep still didn't come her way. It was a long time before daylight only to discover in her dream she was running away from Larry. She wanted to be safe back in her little hiding place, in her own little world all by herself.

Kara was awakened with the sound of the telephone ringing. She had imagined the phone was ringing in her dream. But the phone was definitely ringing and not in her sleep. For hours she gazed at the clock. She thought she had overslept, gasped with anger, and she saw the clock only read six o'clock. She was reaching for the phone. She lay back against the pillow with the receiver pressed against her ear.

"Hello?"

Her voice came out very thick with heavy sleep, and there was a pause before the voice at the other end replied.

"Did I wake you from a nice dream, my spring flower?" said Larry.

If she hadn't been properly awake before, she certainly was now. As she sat up in bed.

"Oh, Larry."

She gritted her teeth on the lie she was about to tell. She thought she heard him laugh at the other end of the phone.

"Larry, I was just making a pot of coffee."

"Kara, you're not good at lying," he rasped. "Now come on, my little spring flower. Don't be ashamed to admit that you were dreaming about me. I only wish I had been there to wake you in person. I would have taken my time at it. Kara are you still with me?"

"Yes, Larry. I'm still here. I take it you have a very good reason for this phone call so early in the morning, Mr. Grant."

"Now, come on, a moment ago you were calling me Larry," he said.

"Okay, I was thinking," she said briskly. "You did take me by surprise."

"Now, my sweet flower, I must do this more often. In fact, I like the idea of waking you up very slowly just to see the look of sweet, sexy pleasure in your brown eyes," said Larry.

"I'm afraid you have two long weeks."

She broke off almost choking slightly as she realized what she had just said to Larry.

He made a slight sound which might have been him laughing at her again.

"Say now, you really want me to be very honest with you?"

Kara had just walked right into it. Larry kind of changed the subject.

"I do have to get ready for work."

Soundless.

"Do you care to tell me your reason for this obscene phone call at this ungodly hour of the morning?"

"Kara?"

"Yes, Larry."

"I promise you there's nothing at all obscene about what I have in mind to do to you one of these days. You will see making love is something to be learned and lingered over. Then, I will know how to help you get back the six years you lost behind your man. Kara, I love very deeply."

"You are stepping on some dangerous ground with me," said Larry.

Kara was trying to keep herself in control. Her breathing was very deep.

"I'll be sure to remember that when that day comes," said Kara. "Mr. Larry, will you forgive me. Like I said, I do have a job to go to. I have a busy day. I only have three days to get this big account in order and get ready for the cruise," said Kara.

She sensed he was suddenly angry. There was a momentary pause before he said another word.

"Hi. Larry. Are you still there?"

"Yes, I'm still here. The reason I called you so early was to find out whether or not you would have dinner with me this evening around 7:30. Or would you prefer to have it a little later?" asked Larry.

Kara gasped, "Larry, we didn't have a date for this evening that I know anything about."

"Oh, you're right, my sweet thing. But you can't have lunch with me. I suggest we talk about a couple of things, first your family and next discuss the cruise. You know what, Kara? You haven't said much one way or the other. So, I do think we need to talk. I will pick you up for dinner tonight at 7:30. You will be a fool if you don't come. This dinner has something to do with business, also," said Larry.

"Look! Larry, I told you I'm interested," she said very weakly. She was imagining his soft sense of impatience.

"Say don't be a fool? Was that a hint or a threat in his voice? Hey, what do you mean," asked Kara.

"Look here, Kara, I'll pick you up at 7:30. I have already booked a table for us."

Kara drew in an angry breath.

"Make it eight o'clock," she said. "I will need the extra time to sharpen my claws."

He was laughing.

"Don't bother, Kara. Just come as you are with your sweet, loving, natural self," said Larry.

Kara slammed the phone down. Tonight at 7:30. Kara sat on the bed again too stunned to take in the full implications of his words. Straight away, she swallowed hard.

"Why do I get the distinct feeling I'm being threatened. This man is moving too fast for me. He didn't ask what time or if I would like to go out. He just told me. I can't imagine his voice implying he can just say I'll pick you up at seven-thirty. Oh yeah, I also booked us a table. Yeah right. Your time, not my time."

If she was going to survive this man she would have to start making her own rules. She hurried to the bathroom to turn on the shower.

The phone was already ringing the minute she walked into the office. She hung up her jacket, sat at the desk, and took several deep breaths before flipping the switch on the intercom.

"Yes, Mrs. Baker."

"Good morning Jenny. Don't put any calls through to me until further notice. Jenny, please just take all the messages. I will get back to whoever it was at a later time. I have to make several business calls and make some contracts. I also have to draw up and book some cruises. My day will be full with the international hotel. Jenny, I need you to call Mr. Luke's secretary. I need to talk with him."

Kara pulled a folder from a stack of files. She was studying the paper. She worked all morning. She buzzed the intercom on her desk.

"Jenny, I'm still waiting for that call from the Greek International. What's the hold up? I'm due to go out in about half an hour."

"I'm still trying but Mr. Luke's secretary insists he's still unavailable."

"Okay, thank you."

"Kara."

"Yes."

"Do you want me to keep trying?"

"No, that's alright. Look, why don't you go for lunch now and take an extra half an hour. You wanted to do some shopping. The meeting is scheduled for an hour, so you go, and I will sort some things out," said Kara.

The rest of the day Kara forced herself to concentrate on her work. By the time she finally reached for her coat and bag, her neck muscles were stiff with lots of tension. She's on her way through the outer office. She dropped a pile of letters onto the desk.

"These are all signed, Jenny. I'm going home a little early. I think one of my migraines is coming on."

Jenny was already rising from behind her desk.

"You do look a little on the pale side. Can I get you anything? Some aspirins maybe?" said Jenny.

Kara shook her head and wished she had waved because the pain increased until it was like a tight band was around her forehead.

"No thank you, Jenny. I have some medication at home. I'll take some as soon as I get home."

She looked at her watch and had some difficulty focusing on the tiny face.

"Look Jenny, why don't you go home yourself. There's nothing to do that can't wait until tomorrow, is there? And by the way, you did say that you had a date right?" Kara asked.

"Yes, I do. Well, that's good. Good night," said Kara.

"Kara, thank you. I hope you will feel much better in the morning."

Kara smiled at Jenny and walked out to her car. She climbed into her car and drove home through some very heavy traffic. This was going to be one of the bad migraines. She hadn't had one like this in a very long time. She made it home safe. She went straight through the house to her bedroom drawing the curtains, shutting out the light before she made herself some coffee. She swallowed two of the strong pain killers, the prescription from her doctor. With a bit of luck, they would make the pain bearable, and she would sleep. Lying awake at night was

one of the things she had become frightened with. Kara made it into the
bedroom. She stepped into the steaming, hot water hoping that would
take away some of the stiffness and tension. She could relax a little.

The doorbell rang. She was talking to herself. She would
ignore it. Whoever it was may soon go away. She lay back in the
scented bubbles and closed her eyes to block out the pain which was
tightened like a steel band around her forehead. The doorbell rang
again. This time, longer and more insistently as if the caller was becoming very angry.

Kara first slammed with annoyance against the bathtub as she
dragged herself out of the water and put her robe over her wet body.
Whoever it was better have a good reason.

"Oh no! Not you."

For several seconds she was shock.

"What are you doing here?"

His dark eyes slowly roamed over her face.

"My sweet little flower, we have a date at 7:30. And by my
time, it's 7:35 now."

"Oh my God, Larry! I had a hard day. I'm tired, and I have
one of my splitting headaches. So what exactly is it you want to talk
about Larry," said Kara.

"Like I said, we still have some unfinished business to discuss.
Now it's time."

His closeness was having a strange effect on her nerves. His
aftershave was also doing a thing to her body. She was a little surprised
to discover that her hands were actually shaking.

"Look, I really don't think there's any need or point in us
talking tonight, Mr. Grant. I think we could talk another day. His hand
reaching out and gripping her wrist in a vice, his name is Larry, damn
you, Kara. My father is Mr. Grant. So why don't you use it now," said
Larry.

"Hey! As you wish. After all what is your name? Oh yeah,
Larry."

"A great deal when you say it, Ms. Kara. I like the sound of it."

Kara released her hand from his tight grip as she found herself
jerked against his muscular frame.

"I'm wondering just what you'll do. As I said, we need to talk,
and this is the time. And we will talk tonight," said Larry.

She laughed bitterly.

"I was under the impression that that was a threat rather than a
statement. And I don't respond to threats," answered Kara.

His eyes looked dangerously.

"Suppose we find out," said Larry.

Kara's lips parted in a furious protest which died as his mouth came and captured hers. In a slow, ruthless kiss, she gasped at the sheer sensuality of it. She was too stunned to retaliate or resist as he sensed it.

Larry groaned softly, drawing her closer. His hand moved lightly against her hair, her cheeks, and then the soft mound of her breasts. A flame of passion so unexpected ran through her that she had to gasp involuntarily. As his lips moved lower and lower, still finding spots of pleasure that she didn't even knew existed until now. He lowered her on the sofa and went down with her. His hands pushing aside the soft fabric of the thin robe.

"Dear God," he rasped. "You're more beautiful than I imagined."

He was kissing every part of her body. His mouth was moving slowly to her stomach. She could feel the hard strength of his thigh against her leg, bruising her flesh. He was moaning hastily.

"I want you. I want to make love to you as much as you want me, too."

"No," the strangled cry of protest came as the sound of his voice had brought her back to earth.

She was on another planet.

"Kara."

"Yes."

Larry was holding her prisoner.

"You do want me. My God, Kara, do say something."

She realized that her own fingers had torn open the buttons of his shirt. She would have gone on to the other planet. The thought was too mortifying to consider. She had to get a hold of herself. Every ounce of her strength was getting weak, lacking of power. Kara had to push him away. Her cheeks were burning as she pulled her robe over her nakedness.

He eased himself back on the sofa. He just looked at her with a raw agony.

"Okay, what's wrong now Kara? What is it?"

She just shook her head. Her eyes were shut tightly in an attempt to hold back the tears. For a brief second, she had wanted him to make lover to her. Like that wild, crazy love, an uncontrolled way, no turning around. Her heart was throbbing. She was struggling to regain control of her emotions.

Larry shifted his weight above hers.

"You're lying, Kara. I don't know why, but you're really lying to me."

She couldn't bring herself to look at him. As she pushed him away, she was getting up from the sofa. She was hugging the robe for protection. Hell, it was too late for that now. He already knew everything about her body, more than she knew, or had imagined herself.

For a while, he had actually made her forget the vow she had made to herself, that it could never happen again. For instance, falling in love again. It only brought nothing but a bunch of heartache. She had already had more than her fair share of that. What she had failed to take into account was she wouldn't meet someone like Larry Grant, and, last, her own body might betray her.

"Kara, in the name of God, what is the matter with you?"

He was on his feet refastening his shirt. As he came toward her, she warned him off.

"Don't, please don't touch me."

Larry stopped in his tracks. He made no attempt to move any closer. The turmoil in her eyes seemed a warning. Enough that if he did, she would take off running.

"Look Kara, I wouldn't hurt you, not for anything. You must know that by now."

Kara just stared at him through a haze of pain as her head seemed to be gripped by a band of steel drums.

"Look Mr. Larry, let's just forget it ever happened. It certainly won't ever happen again. That's for sure," explained Kara.

Larry just stood and looked at her in confusion.

"Do you still love that man that much?"

For an instance, Kara stared at him. She drew a ragged breath. My God! The man is assuming that I have rejected him because she was clinging on to her old memories of Mike. Hell with Mike, he had gradually killed any remaining feelings of love she might have had in the month before he left. He had changed so much that the only emotions he had aroused in her was fear, pity, and finally sadness for what he had become. No one knew that she sure wasn't going to tell anybody about it.

Larry realized that was her best defense against him.

"Larry, I suggest you draw your own conclusions, and I'll do likewise. Then forget what just happened. Just as I intend to do. She turned away from him."

"Say Kara, maybe I don't want to forget."

He caught her and pulled her to him roughly so he could look her in the face. She swallowed hard.

"I'm afraid you don't have much of a choice."

She focused her gaze on him very aware of the steel strength of his body against her thigh. She tried to break away from him. A man like Larry Grant, you sure ain't too safe to keep at a long arm length.

"I told you, I'm not interested."

"Correction," he said. "Look, sweet thing, I think I just prove that to be incorrect to both of our satisfaction, whether or not you care to admit it. So I won't accept that you still love your husband because I don't believe it."

Kara suddenly had a sharp pain in her chest.

"My feelings for my husband has nothing to do with you."

"Oh, my sweet thing, I say they have a great deal to do with me."

"Kara, when you begin to realize I'm flesh and blood and no memory in this world can make you feel the way you did just now," explained Larry.

"Yes, right. But it won't happen again Mr. Grant. That's a promise. Just put it down as a sudden moment of weakness," said Kara. "Sure, call it what you like Kara, but don't make promises you can't keep, and I certainly don't intend to keep. So stop punishing yourself," Larry said with a smile.

Kara moved quickly to the door and jerked it open.

"I think it's time for you to leave. You got what you come for," said Kara.

"Now Kara, I wouldn't say that. As a matter of fact," he took an envelope from his inner jacket pocket and tossed it onto the coffee table, "This is the real reason I came. I really did mean to talk to you about some business. I told you I had your best interest at heart. Perhaps you should read that through really well," said Larry.

"What is it?" said Kara.

Looking at his face and back of the envelope.

"Why not read it. It's a draft report drawn up by our lawyers and counselor experts on hotels and other facilities like Mr. Luke Adam, the Greek International."

"Oh no! I've been trying to reach that man all day, and his secretary kept saying he was out."

"Yes, right, everyone has a price. Mine was the right amount," said Kara.

He raised an eyebrow.

"Kara, I am interested in knowing you."

This man was deliberately challenging her, and her blood was boiling mighty hot. Whatever it is, you certainly could meet as she looked at the envelope.

"What makes you think I'll be interested in what's in the

envelope?"

"Well my sweet little thing, I don't think you will be able to resist the challenge."

"You're right Mr. Grant. Some things are easier to resist than others."

He just burst out laughing.

"Not this one, Mrs. Baker. Just look through the plans and think about it. We can discuss your ideas over lunch tomorrow. I'll pick you up around one o'clock."

She threw him one of her evil eyes.

"Look Larry, I'm on a diet."

The phone rang. So much for an early night, she thought. Who on earth could be calling her now?

"You can show yourself out. I know you are able to do that."

She looked at Larry and picked up the phone, turning her back deliberately on him.

"I'll wait until you finish," he said softly. "I do hate to leave on an incomplete note."

Kara uncovering the phone mouthpiece.

"Yes!" She snapped.

"Hello Kara. This is Drew. I haven't called at a bad time have I?"

"Oh no, Drew. No, no of course you haven't called at a bad time."

Her face lit up with pleasure. But the look that Larry gave her, a sudden look of anger which swept across his face.

"Kara, you sound a little tense. I'm sorry if I interrupted something."

"Drew, you are not interrupting a thing."

She glanced at Larry with a hint of mischief.

"As a matter of fact Drew, I was a little bored. I promised myself an early night with a good book."

She looked at Larry with a smile. Larry's arm came around her waist, and he spoke with a cool whisper in her ear.

"You won't be needing any book, darling, not if I have anything to say in the matter, my sweet thing," said Larry.

Kara covered the mouthpiece quickly throwing him a look of anger. He had done that deliberately knowing very well that Drew could hear him. Now he was smiling like the cat had got the damn milk.

She picked the phone up and moved as far away from Larry as she could.

Drew was saying to Kara, "I hope I haven't interrupted anything. Did I call at a bad time? I didn't realize you had someone with you," said Drew.

"Oh stop being silly," she snapped. "I told you it's not important."

"Well, okay, Kara. Actually I called to ask if you would have lunch with me at 12:00 p.m. tomorrow. I still feel troubled about what happened to you. So I would like a chance to explain my side," said Drew.

"There's really no need to," said Kara. "Well, I still would like to make the record straight. You know things were more or less taken out of my hands. You know Mr. Grant is the sort of man that lets nothing or nobody stand in his way. He will step right on the little man."

Kara looked at Larry. He had heard every word Drew had said about him.

"Drew, that sounds like a great idea about lunch tomorrow. I would like it very much."

She looked in Larry's direction.

"I'm sure we have a lot to talk about," said Kara. "Until tomorrow then. Same place as usual."

She hung up the phone.

"So Ms. Kara, my company bores you."

His hand was moving on her back. He was drawing her closer to him.

"Please, it will be a mutual pleasure. That I promise, my sweet thing."

She was looking at him. Then his knee gently forced her leg apart.

"No!"

"Yes, Kara. Yes."

His voice was a soft muffled sound in her ear. His hand was in her hair as he was kissing her throat.

"I want you, and you want me. Say it damn, admit it!"

His hand removed her robe exposing her shoulder and breasts. His hand moved slowly all over her body until she cried out, her body arching against the hard of his thighs. Oh yes she wanted and needed it, but not now.

"Say it!" He was commanding her. "Say I want you, Larry."

She was fighting him so hard. The affect he was having on her was taking every ounce of her strength that was left in her weak body. If he only knew the power he already had on her to the point whereas she forgot all her sanity. Her body was receiving all that sensual pleasure.

His hand was sending both desire and fear all through her body. Yes, she had no doubt he wanted her. He had already warned her that sooner or later he always got just what he wanted. She was loving that sweet taste on his lips. She was thinking how many women had he made love to like this and walked away never looking back. Her breath came in sharp as she pushed him away from her.

"Oh, my God, you sure know how to throw a mean curve a man's way. But my sweet love, your body was just talking to me just now. It was sending out all kinds of signs as he looked at her. His eyes had that darken angry look. Kara, I don't think you have the faintest idea what you do to me. Hell, if you did you would stop playing all the dangerous childless game."

She was shaken by the discovery. She managed to walk to the door and hold it open.

"Good night, Mr. Grant. I'm sorry I couldn't make it tonight."

He paused at the door.

"One of these days I will break through those difficult walls of yours, Ms. Kara. So you better watch out, my sweet flower."

She swallowed hard, "Is that another one of your threat."

"No, that's a promise," he said softly. "Don't forget to look through those plans. Sleep my love and sweet dreams. I'll be in touch."

She made no attempt to answer. She closed the door behind him. She locked it and stood for a moment breathing deeply. She shook her head knowing that what he said was so true, but she couldn't go through the pain and punishment of loving and losing someone all over again. Her indifference was far too strongly built to be in any danger from a man like that. He was an arrogant man and completely ruthless, the kind of man who believed that simply because he wanted something it had to happen right then.

The headache had gone, and the last thing she wanted was to go to bed. The bath water was cold now. She walked over to the TV set to watch something on TV. She went from one channel to another before finally giving up and switching it off.

Oh yes, the envelope Larry had dropped off. After all she could at least look at it. She did need a new company and contract from Mr. Luke Adams. Larry had already talked to the man. Now if she accepted it, she walked over to the sofa and picked up the envelope. Sitting down on the sofa she tucked her leg up beside her and began to read the contract Larry had left for her to look over without even thinking about it. She reached for a pen and sketch pad and begin making notes. If she accepted this job, she would have to accept Mr. Larry Grant as a controlling all consuming. That would mean all accounts like this one could bring her business up to standards. Hell, she sure couldn't afford to turn it down. She got ready for bed.

CHAPTER FOUR

"Good morning, my sweet flower. Did I awake you again this morning? Did you read the report I left with you? I hope so."

"Yes, I did, but Larry, I never told you anything about my business or anything about a contract with Mr. Luke Adams nor about the International Hotel ever," said Kara.

"You're right," he said. "We never talked business. What I'm suggesting is strictly a business contract. So Kara, we do have a great deal to talk about. It's just you are afraid to step out in the world. If not, what have you got to lose?"

"Yes, Larry." Quite a lot she thought.

"Yes, but can you afford to turn it down," asked Larry.

"What do you mean," asked Kara.

"Look here, Kara. You must have weighed the pros and cons. Take it all into account the kind of financial success an account like this could bring you. And think about the nice rewards. Or perhaps you intend on spending the rest of your life wasting your undoubted talents in a business which hardly does you any justice. A business you are just tick ticking along but will never make a fortune."

She was shaking with shock. Her eyes blazing with anger.

"Larry, you've been checking up on me! I'm running a damn good business. So what gives you the right to check up on my business? You certainly don't have that right Mr. Grant."

"Kara, I don't make any kind of mistakes. And I certainly don't take chances. I always check things out beforehand."

"Yeah, right, Larry. This might be one of those days you have pushed the wrong button. I'm a small business. If I decide to do a contract, why me? There must be about a dozen other travel agents that are more qualified. Now Larry, would you like to tell me your reason?" asked Kara.

"You're right. There's that lazily drawled word which took her breath away."

"Then who?"

"Oh, come now, my sweet flower. Can't you guess by now? It's not that hard, my love."

Hell, that was the trouble already. Her imagination was running wild and crazy. As it was she didn't need to think at all. She was having all kinds of worried dreams. She had to have strength to deal with this man.

"Well, my love, since you will not tell me, I will pick you up for dinner tonight at 7:30. You'll be a fool not to come this time my love."

She was sure she heard him laugh or was it perhaps a cry of rage. Either way she decided to hurry to the bathroom to turn on the shower. Larry Grant was one pain in the neck. He was pushing me too many ways. If she wanted to survive, she was going to start making her own rules to be able to stand in the same world with Mr. Grant.

Kara was having one of those mornings. She was late for work, and the phone had been ringing most of the morning. The traffic had been heavy, and she was running behind time, but she was only a little late.

Kara stood in the doorway of the crowded wine bar. She was looking for Drew. The room was filled with smoke. She couldn't see until her eyes became adjusted to the light. Then she saw Drew. She was walking in his direction. She went toward him with a smile on her face. She was completely unrewarded that she had drawn a lot of attention to herself. She was only in to see Drew. She had on a cool linen skirt with a matching jacket and a jade color blouse gave quite a stunning look. She was totally unknowing the eyes she was getting at the time.

Drew was looking also with a half smile on his face. He had already bought drinks. His glass was empty. Her glass of orange juice was waiting for her. Drew knew her taste. He didn't need to ask what she wanted. He kissed her on the check as she made her way to the table.

"Kara, I was afraid you weren't going to make it."

Kara settled into the seat tucking her bag down by her feet and drew a breath of air.

"Drew, the traffic was heavy. I'm really sorry I'm late, but something came up. It was rather urgent and by the time I tried to reach you, but you had already left the office."

She bit her lip knowing all along she was not telling the whole story. Not telling about Larry who had got her day off to such a bad start, and she had spent most of the morning trying to get back on schedule.

Now she was sensing agony in Drew. She forced herself to smile.

"You know something Drew, I was looking forward to this little outing. The noisy bar and the good food, I guess I am going to have to run around the block a couple of times."

She began to laugh. She hoped she would be forgiven for this lie.

"Kara, I know how it is. I'm just glad you made it especially under the circumstances. Perhaps we better order, or we might not get any lunch."

He shot her a curious look. Kara was a little puzzled by his words. What could he possibly mean under the circumstances? What the hell was Drew talking about? Drew was looking at his watch.

"So, Kara, I'm afraid I have to be back in an hour. You know it's like everyone is afraid to step on the new boss' toes.

Kara laughed.

"My Drew, I hadn't realized you were so untrying."

Drew grinned, "Yes, new management and all that. There's a lot going on. Not that I'm complaining," he said quickly.

Almost too quick.

Kara said, "I guess it will be kind of hard to give up the extended lunch breaks."

Which she knew from experience. Lunch had often run into mid-afternoon. She and Drew ordered lunch. When they had finished ordering the waiter brought her coffee. She put cream and sugar in her coffee. She stirred the coffee and sat back with a sigh of satisfaction.

"You know, Drew, I have always liked this place, but I try to avoid this bar because if not, I would be on a diet every week."

Drew was looking at the slender curves of her figure in a way that was making her a little uncomfortable. But at least he didn't leave her feeling that she had been mentally stripped completely naked the way Larry Grant looked at her. Yet she was sensing an odd hint which was starting to puzzle her she guessed.

"The reason I asked you to lunch, Kara," said Drew.

"Oh, Drew! I hope you're not still worrying about what happened," said Kara.

Drew said wearily, "Well, I'm blaming myself because I didn't get the contract with Mr. Grant. I don't hold you responsible. I hope you know that," said Kara.

For a moment Drew just looked very uncomfortable.

"You know I couldn't blame you if you thought that, I swear

Kara. My hands were tied until everything was signed and sealed. We were all sworn to secrecy. Everything was confidential, and if anyone broke it, they would suffer the consequences."

His hand ran through his hair.

"Kara, I couldn't afford to lose my job, and that's what it would have meant," said Drew.

"I understand your position. I would have done the same thing."

She gave him a tight smile knowing only too well just how ruthless Mr. Ryan O'Neal could be at times.

"Like he owns the world," said Kara.

"Well, I thought you might feel like I owe something to you like loyalty, that is," said Drew.

Kara was unable to help him with whatever battle it was that he was fighting.

"Drew!" she snapped impatiently. "Whatever else it is just let the matter drop."

"Oh Kara, I supposed, I imagined we had some sort of a relationship. That was my mistake in which case, I'm sorry," said Drew.

"My God, man, what are you talking about? We are just good friends," said Kara.

"Well, I suppose I should be grateful for that at least. I guess I've been pretty naïve in hoping it might be more. Hell, Kara I thought you were off limits to men in general. I had figured it was just me. You should have told me how it was between you and Mr. Larry Grant," he laughed bitterly. "Believe me I know I can't win against that sort of man. This is a lost competition. I would never in a million years thought you would talk to a man like Grant. Damn Kara, he's a woman lover. He must have used some pretty powerful persuasion on you. Look Kara, what else I'm suppose to think knowing that he spent the night at your place," said Drew.

Kara licked her lips telling herself this was some kind of a nightmare.

"What exactly makes you think that I didn't hear the man in the background last night? Why in heaven's name didn't you tell me you had someone with you when I phoned? Kara, the last thing I wanted was to cause you any embarrassment. First it was six years without a man, now you are off to the island for two weeks with a man."

"Wait one minute, Mr. Drew. How did you know I was about to take a trip to some island as you said? Would you like to tell me who in the world told you that? I sure don't remember telling you about a trip. Sure as hell not one thing to anybody about a man in my life. So

Drew, would you like to be the one to tell me who is telling you about
my business in the first place?" said Kara.

"Kara, come on now, your Mr. Grant was the one. He met me
this morning at work and nicely told me in so many words that you
were his woman. He also made it clear that you were not just some
friend to him. So like I said, I'm very sorry to have interfered in your
life. But Kara, you are moving mighty fast with this man."

Without waiting for her to reply, he turned and walked away,
leaving her standing, looking shocked and outraged.

"The man is just my friend, not my lover."

Now here Drew is mad with her about Larry Grant. He told
Drew all about our relationship. She was making her way back to her
car.

Another day all messed up for her. She was now heading back
to the office to try to do some work. She needed to work on some new
documents and some more paperwork that needed to be taken care of
before the day was over.

Kara was sitting in a chair looking out the window, just looking
at Larry. The doorbell rang, in fact it rang a few more times before Kara
went to answer it. She started not to answer it for one simple reason.
She knew that if she didn't, he would keep on ringing it or break the
door down. She opened the door with half a smile.

"Where the hell were you?" he rasped. "I know you heard the
doorbell ringing."

"Oh yes! I sure as hell did. It would have been kind of hard not
to. The way you were acting. Matter-of-fact, I was trying hard to get
dressed before you came over," said Kara.

"Now, my sweet thing, let's not push the wrong button, not
tonight. You are not ready for that. It could be a problem. You still
have to realize I play the same game you are trying to play. Right now
to save you a lot of problems, I can solve it for you right now by
dressing you myself. I would love to do that for you now. Is that a yes
or no?" asked Larry.

"No, Mr. Larry, but you do need to solve this problem. What
did you say to Drew? Today we had lunch together. He said you told
him something about I was your woman in so many words. Did you
say something like that Larry?"

CHAPTER FIVE

"Oh, my sweet thang, you never allow anyone to interfere in your life. Now your safety is my concern," said Larry. "Now, my little flower, everybody plays a fool sometimes. You don't even know that the man is madly in love with you. Try to remember ain't no shame with my game at all baby."

Kara was standing with her mouth wide open. No sound was coming out.

He looked at Kara saying, "Try not to misunderstand me. I do not stand at anyone's crossroads or play second best to anyone. Like I say, my rule is the only way or no way at all."

Kara walked out of the living room into her bedroom. She was thinking how confused she was right now. First it was Drew. Now here comes Mr. Larry talking about a relationship we never even talked about. What's next? She walked into her closet to get a dress. She put on an ivory-colored, tailored suit with some bone colored shoes, and a little makeup, but not that much. She walked back out to Larry.

He said, "I thought I was going to have to check up on your examination to make sure everything was under control."

He started laughing at Kara. She didn't see anything so funny.

She said, "Let's go, Larry."

Then walked out of the house. She locked the door and walked to the car. Larry opened the door for her.

Arriving at the restaurant, the waiter ushered them to a table. The waiter took their order. Larry was looking at Kara.

"Now that I have gotten you out the house, my love, let's talk about your life and family. Since I have to meet the other half of the Bakers on Sunday, I think I need to know something about them. I already know John. We run across one another at Willie's house from time to time. He is a nice young man. So tell me about the rest of the family," said Larry with a smile.

The waiter returned with the food.

"Let's talk and eat. You know life is a gamble."

Kara looked at Larry, "You know something. My son never ever told me that he already knew you until the other day. He stated that he had met you. Before he was laughing telling me he had already met you. Anyway, my son, John, is kind. He takes after his uncle Willie. By being a doctor, he specializes only on babies. He also likes medicine. He is a very good doctor. Now, my older one, Brian, he's married with two adorable children, a boy and a girl. He is also a district attorney. His wife Mary is a judge. Brian is also my lawyer. My girl, Carol, she runs around behind her Aunt Pam. She is a model. She also has her own modeling school. She models in Paris. All of her aunt's clothes for her shop she brought in Paris. The last of the bunch is Diane. She is my sweetest one. She is very precious to me. She never talks much. She always looks and listens to you talk. She specializes with the brain and the mind. She is the brain of the family. She is a physician. She still doesn't talk that much unless you make her angry. Then you will have a big mess on your hands. Now that's my family and my life," said Kara.

"Now Kara, I would like to know more about you my love. There's something you are leaving out."

"But Larry, my family is my life. Also, my son and your best friend have told you all about the countdown," said Kara with a half smile.

"Look! Larry, tonight you wanted me to tell you all about my life, but to me it looks like you already are ahead of the game. My son and friend have told my life stories to you already, I think. So Larry, there's nothing else to tell you about my little life."

"Now look at me, Kara. You listen to me. I keep on telling you to play by my own golden rule. So please try to remember that I'm no second hand man. So talk to me, little one."

"Larry, Yes. Would you order me some coffee?"

"Of course, my love."

He called the waiter over and ordered some coffee and cheese-cake. The waiter returned back with her coffee and cheese cake.

"Now you have my full attention," said Larry.

"Well, my childhood was very good. I have a big brother. It was just the two of us. My parents were not wealthy, but we lived a happy life. In our house was lots of love. My mother was a teacher at the university. My father was the community dentist. My parents are retired now. They travel a lot. They are traveling across the state. My brother and I help keep them traveling. We lived in a small community called a social unit. We all were friendly associates. Everybody worked.

No one was home. Pam, Helen, and I lived close together in the community. The three of us went to the same school and college. We were called the Jersey Girls. We were tied and bonded together. We got engaged and married about the same time. Pam and Helen are still married and living happily. You know the rest about me," said Kara.

"Look baby, you are going to leave all those old memories behind and come back to the living world with me. We will walk down that happy road together. I want you to laugh more, baby. Let your hair down, and enjoy life again. Your, Mr. Right is right here. Look at you. I have everything under control and that's a promise. I'm no mistake."

"Oh right, Mr. Larry. Don't make any promises you can't keep. I've already had that. Now take me home."

Together they walked to the car.

"Kara did you make up your mind about the document I gave you the other day. I know you."

"I haven't had enough time to think about it," says Kara.

"Just try not to take too long about it. Okay?" asked Larry.

"Yes, I thought about it, but I gave it to my lawyer. He will let you know something Larry. This is the first time I have talked about anything in my life before. That makes me feel really good."

He pulled up in front of the house. Larry got out and walked around the car and opened the door. They walked to the house together. "Kara, my love, he moved his hand up her back and to her shoulder, to her throat."

His hands spread into her hair, clasping her head and holding her still beneath his kiss.

He said, "Good night, my love, and walked away."

She walked inside the house with a smile on her face tonight. He had taken her in his arms with one hot kiss. With hot liquid running all through her body, she stood before the mirror in her bedroom looking at her swollen lips.

She walked into the shower thinking, "This man was getting too close. Relax."

He said life is a gamble.

"Yeah, but I still never have time. I truly don't have too much faith in men right now. She needed to sleep on this and get lots of sleep, too."

Sunday morning Kara was getting everything ready for the Sunday dinner. She was getting ready to bake a chocolate cake, two sweet potato pies, and a cheesecake. She marinated her meat for about two hours. The phone was ringing. She picked up the receiver. She heard her mother's voice.

"Hello, my baby. We are back home. Your father wants to come over so that you can prepare breakfast for him. Baby, we are at the airport. Your brother is here to bring us home. May we all come over for breakfast?"

"Yes, mom. Why would you ask me that? You never need an invitation to come to my house. I'll start right on breakfast. Father still likes his favorite, old-fashioned breakfast with everything?"

"Yes. You're right. All that fat food. Kara, we will be over there in about an hour. Love you baby."

"I love you, too, mother."

She hung up the phone. Immediately after hanging up the phone, it rang again. She picked up the phone. It was Pam.

"So, my love, what does this call mean? I know it can't mean you are not coming over today."

"Oh no! Mrs. Thang. I'm calling to make sure you're still having dinner. We are not courting at all today!" she smiled.

"Yes, Pam, we are still having dinner. Guess what? My parents came home this morning. My brother is at the airport right now picking them up. My father wants me to make breakfast for him. So they will be coming over in about an hour from now. I was getting ready to make my cakes and pies, but now I have to do breakfast and dinner all in one."

"So Kara, I picked up two bottles of Champagne for your dinner. I will keep it on ice until dinner. Kara, before I forget to ask, did my baby get back from Paris yet?"

"Yes, Pam, your baby asked about you. She came in about two this morning. She went straight to bed. She said something about a package for her mom Pam. Something about Paris anyway. She's asleep now."

"Well, good. She will tell me all about it when I see her today," said Pam.

"Yes, love, I'm sure she will. It's been good talking to you, but I have to go now. Talk to you later on today, good-bye," said Kara.

She needed to go to the store. She didn't have everything she needed to cook for her father's favorite breakfast. He was an old-fashioned breakfast guy.

She didn't have time to cook and go to the store. She decided to call John.

"John, please be at home this morning."

She dialed John's number. The phone rang a couple of times and on the third ring he answered.

"Hello, Mom."

"John, I kneed you to go to the store for me. Your grandparents are back in town. I need some food to cook breakfast for daddy this morning. I need it right now. Will you get dressed and go for me? I need everything. I'm out of sausage, bacon, and eggs. I need the works. You and Ms. 'Cute-thang' can come also and have breakfast. I heard her in the background. I'll see you in about thirty minutes. Good-bye, son."

CHAPTER SIX

"I sure don't need anymore phone calls. I need some help right now! Well, my little sweet, you have got to get up this morning because I need you, right now!"

She dialed Diane's number. The phone rang about four times before she picked the phone up.

"Yes, Mom. What is your big problem," said Diane?

"My Godchild, why is it every time I call you, you think it's always a problem?" said Kara?

"Well, mom, because when you call usually it's a problem, or you need me to do something for you this early in the morning. You know I am still in bed. I'm trying so hard to relax before this evening, mom. I need a clear head to be surrounded by your tribe. You know everybody is trying to talk at one time. Especially that son of yours, Mr. Lawman with his injustice. He always has to have the floor. We always have court and jury day. And poor little Mary, she's the judge. She works all day as a judge, then she comes home to that fool of a husband of hers has her as a judge again. With that man around, what a life! Nevertheless, mom, what is your big problem?" asked Diane.

"Well, my love, your sweet little grandparents are back. They are on their way home right now from the airport."

"Mother, that's the best news I've heard today. Thank the Lord for granddaddy. That way Mr. Lawman won't be having the floor today, how sweet! Paw-paw will tell Mr. Lawman we will not be having any court here today. He will say, "Boy, save that for tomorrow at your job! How sweet it is! This is my day, mom. So, what's on your book for me? I'm ready," said Diane.

"Okay my love. Your paw-paw wants me to cook breakfast for him this morning. I need your help. Will you be so nice and come over and help me out. This way I can start on Sunday's dinner. I need you to get dressed and make your way home in about forty-five minutes.

Thank you. Bye now."

She hangs up the phone.

"Well, that's all taken care of. As soon as John brings the grocery, I can start on breakfast. Now for Ms. Carol with that mouth of hers, she's the one I sure can do without right now. She needs to get all the sleep she can get. If she doesn't get her rest, she will get up raising all kinds of hell. Without her rest, she is a no-no."

"My daddy still likes his homemade biscuits. It's been a very long time since I made homemade biscuits. I do hope I can still handle the job. He likes lots of bacon, sausage, country ham, cheese soufflé, grits, and hot coffee. Now that's what I call a good old-fashioned breakfast. This morning mom said that everything was too fat. Well, he's her husband. He's just my father and the boss in my book. Now my dinner. I need to start on the meats: veal, pot roast, and roast duck. That takes longer than the vegetables. The rest can wait for a little while. Daddy comes first this morning. Time keeps on moving."

"John, you're here! That's good. Now I can start on breakfast. Did you bring "Miss Cutie" with you?"

"Yes, Mom. That little "Miss Cutie's" name is Lillian," said John. "She will help you in the kitchen, if you need her. And yes, mom, she's the right one this time."

"John, I'm so glad to hear that. I would love to have two more babies and another daughter-in-law. Which one of these pictures should I be looking at for another Miss Cutie of a daughter-in-law?"

She was laughing at John.

"Okay, mom. You can have fun on my special day," said John.

"Oh thank you, son. Now you and Lillian can set the table. Oh by the way, when is the other part of the family going to meet Ms. Lillian," asked Kara?

"My, my, Mr. John Baker, I didn't think you told me that you knew Mr. Larry until I told the family about the man. Right! Mr. Baker."

John was laughing at this mom.

"You're right about that. Because the way you talked about a man, I just knew that Larry wouldn't last a week until you would have hung the man up by his behind. But the man is still around with a big smile on his face. Now mom, that's one bad man. He walks right in and took over. Now talk about my kind of man, mom, he's already got my vote. Uncle Willie says he's been around a very long time, so I lost the bet, mom. The man is still holding on. He takes my mother, I mean, the sweet woman to the island for two weeks. Mom, I love you. I'm so glad that you're finally going to live your life again. Mom, I'll always have your back all the time," said John.

"Well, thank you, John. Your mother needs to hear that from you. Now that brother of yours, that's a horse of a different color," said Kara.

"Mom, look, don't worry about Brian. Uncle and I have got his back, also. Now that Papa is here, I wouldn't worry."

John and Kara hug. Kara had tears in her eyes.

The doorbell rings. In walks Diana, her mother, father, and brother.

"Mother! I'm so glad to see you. How was your trip? Mother, I talked to you and daddy yesterday. You didn't say anything about coming home."

"I know baby, but your father didn't like the way you were talking about Brian, the man you're dating, and the dinner. Now you know how your father is. So he said to me, let's go home right now. So love, here we are."

"Yes, mom, and we are glad you are here. Big brother, you passed my house and didn't tell me our parents were coming home! How's your family? You need to bring everybody over for dinner today. I have enough for everyone."

"Daddy, are you alright?"

"Yes child, I need to take a little nap while you are cooking. Please call Brian for me, and tell him to come over here. I need to talk with him before the dinner. By the way, where is my little mouthy Carol?"

"She's asleep."

"Well, wake her up. I need to talk with her, too. I'll be in the backroom. This way I can see all my babies at the same time," said father.

"Diane, you look very well, baby. When are you getting married? Come and give your old nanny some sweet little kisses. Diane all my close friends already have about fifteen to twenty grandchildren. Could you give your old grandma a couple of babies?"

"Yes, you're right, Nanny. But wouldn't it be much nicer if I had a man first? Maybe a husband before I start a family," said Diane.

"Well, my child, what are you waiting for? You are not getting any younger, that's for sure. So start looking for someone," said Nanny.

"John, would you like to tell me your reason for not being married. It can't be the money because you are very successful with your job. So what is the hold up? I need you all to stop delaying this. John, is this young lady your friend? Child, what is your name?"

"Lillian Hodges," said Lillian. "John, she's a cute little thing," said Nanny.

"Yes, Nanny, she is my friend, but…"

In walked Carol.

"Well, well, my little brother. At last you brought Lillian home. I guess you brought her to meet the whole tribe. You know John has been seeing her for about two years now, and he's just bringing her now to meet the family. You know one thing about this family. They like to keep little secrets away from the others. My mother and brother, they are two of a kind. They were telling you a thing. John and Lillian have been friends for two years. Lillian is one of my models. Today, he brings her home to the family. So all I can say is it's about time," said Carol.

John looked at Carol and started laughing.

"You know telling you something would not be a secret anymore," said John.

"Alright, you two. So Carol finally you're up. Did you get enough sleep?"

"Yes, mother."

"Good morning, Nanny. It's good to have you and Papa back home. I didn't see Papa."

"Carol, it is good to see you. Your papa is taking a nap before breakfast," said Nanny. "John, is your brother coming over?" asked Nanny.

"Yes, he is on his way."

In walked Brian and his family.

"Good morning, mother, Nanny, and everybody. Who's the new girl?"

"The new girl is John's friend. We will talk about it much later. Right now, breakfast is ready. Go get your papa, Brian. We can eat now."

"Mary, are you still hanging in there with my grandson? And how is the job going for you? We are so proud of you and John. You two have worked so hard to become a judge and a district attorney. You two have made it to the top. Your parents are proud of you, too. I was talking to your mother the other day, and all she could talk about was her little ones and her daughter becoming a judge. We had a good laugh."

"Good morning, everyone. My whole tribe is here. Let's eat."

"I'm starved and looking forward to this country breakfast. My baby girl has cooked for me. So come on everybody let's bless the food," said Papa.

Everyone was sitting down to enjoy a good country breakfast.

CHAPTER SEVEN

Sunday afternoon around two o'clock p.m. everyone was sitting in the den. The Baker family, the Blackwell family, the Nicholas family and the Brown family.

Father Blackwell said, "I really have the whole tribe here today. You know Belinda, it makes me very happy to have all the children together again. It brings back all the memories of those Sundays when the kids would come over to the house and sit, talk, and laugh. Those were the good old days."

"Today is Kara and John's day. John has something to say before the main guest comes to join our family. John the floor is open to you."

"Thank you, Papa. I want to introduce everybody to my friend Lillian Hodges. She is becoming a part of this family in about five months. We are engaged to be married. Nanny, how about giving us a year before a little one comes along? Lillian has to finish out her contract with the agency. She's been touring France for nine months. We can wait a few months to do some traveling for ourselves. Can't we, Nanny?" asked John.

"Son, this calls for a celebration for the two of you. Lillian, you are welcome to enter into this family. Will there be a large wedding?" asked Nanny.

"Yes, Mrs. Blackwell," answered Lillian.

Kara is in the kitchen cooking the dinner for this afternoon. Her son is telling everybody about his plans to be married in five months. As her father said, this is a day to celebrate and to have two more added to the family is just great.

She was checking on dinner. She had cooked veal, pot roast, smothered in mushroom sauce, asparagus casserole, green beans, broccoli with cream cheese, red cabbage and chestnuts, boiled potatoes, duck with orange sauce, wild brown rice, eggplant casserole, and sweet potatoes.

"In walked mother. Why are you walking backward looking out of the window, child? Does the man know the way to the house?" asked mother.

"Yes, mom."

"Well, child, stop and visit with us for awhile. I know how your nerves are, but everything will be alright. Be patient, and things will be better than you think. We came home to make sure of it. Your mother and father are always with you, baby. Willie said this man was a good man. Listen baby, you cried for twenty years over Mike. He was a no count of a husband, but always a good father to the children and still is. That's because he was always running around. Too bad he didn't run to you."

Both of them began to laugh.

"Mother, I have stopped crying. Mom, I'm so glad you and daddy are home. I miss you so much when you all are not home," said Kara.

"Well, my love, you can stop walking backward and walk forward to the front door. I believe your young man is here," said her mother.

Kara walks down the hall to open the front door. Larry was standing there looking so good with a smile on his face.

"Hello, Kara."

"Back to you Larry. Do come in. We're noticing all the cars in the yard. I gather everybody is here. Can I get a kiss before meeting the family?"

Kara answered, "Yes."

He took her in his arms and held her before kissing.

"I need this baby," he said.

He kissed and held her until everybody laughed.

"Good afternoon everyone. Everybody this is Larry Grant. Larry, these are my parents, Mr. and Mrs. Blackwell, my son, Brian, and his wife, Mary, and their two children. Over here are my two daughters, Diane and Carol, and my brother Timothy. This is my best friend, Pam, and her husband, Ronald Brown, my son, John, in which you already know and his friend, Lillian Hodges. The others you already know."

"Yes, I do. We know each other very well, right, Brian?"

"Yeah, we have had some head-butting, some long days, and nights in court."

"Brian! This is the man you were telling us about. The one you would like to lock up?"

"Oh yeah! He's the one, but I sure didn't know he was the one my mother has been seeing for some months. This man likes everything to go his way, or there's no way at all," explained Brian.

"The issue is, I win don't I?" asked Larry.

"Oh yeah, that you do. Changing the subject a little, you're taking my mother to the island for two weeks, right?"

"You're good. She has never been out of the states, hell, let along to some island. So, Mr. Larry, take good care of my mother," said Brian.

"Mr. Brian, I'm the man! I'm taking my woman to the islands, like you said, for two weeks. She will be my responsibility. This lady is the princess of my heart. Brian you don't have anything to worry about, and neither do you Mr. Blackwell. I will take good care of your daughter," said Larry with a smile.

"Well, son, this family is glad to meet you, right, Brian?"

"Yes, Pop," said Brian.

"Good, Kara will be serving the dinner in a few minutes, but, in the meantime, ladies, please close your mouths. Kara, baby, get the glasses. Pam, you go and get the champagne so we can make a toast. We sure need one today. My daughter and my grandson have made this old man's day very happy. My baby girl has finally found someone to care for her. Come on everybody. Get a glass, and let's make a toast to Kara, Larry, John, and Lillian. Your mother and I are giving our praises and best wishes with lots of love and blessings. May God go with you," said Mr. Blackwell.

Kara called everyone to come into the dining room. It was time to serve the dinner. Everyone was seated and ready to have a fun time. Mrs. Belinda looked at Lillian.

"What will you do after your contract expires?" asked Mrs. Belinda.

"Well, Mrs. Belinda, I'm already working with Carol at school. I will take over Carol's school while she's in France," said Lillian.

"Oh! I see," said Mrs. Belinda.

"Ms. Carol is opening a modeling school in France. She asked me to help her run this school here. I will be moving back to the states. Then, I will be much closer to my husband," said Lillian.

"Oh, I see! That is very nice of you to do that," said Mrs. Belinda.

"Carol! We need to talk," said Nanny. "Carol, do you have something to tell your family? If I'm wrong, please put me back on the right side of the road."

"Little sis,' a few hours ago and I quote, if I'm wrong, you said

"This family is always keeping too many secrets from one another." Now this is something. You kept it away from the other half of your family. Little sis', would you be so kind as to explain to the others your nice, little secret? Mom, Pam, and Pop Ronald didn't know about her plans. Pop Ronald was in France two weeks ago. He said he was on some "important business."

"Mom and Pam, please don't look at me that way. I know you are a good mom. All we have to do is pick up the phone, call you or Pop, and you will be right there for us, and keep little secrets, too," said Kara.

Everybody laughed.

"Now back to you, Carol. Wait until the other half of your family hears about your good news," said Diana.

"Look Diane, everything you keep on ice, and I quote is true. I didn't want the family to learn about the school until I had positive proof that everything was on the up and up. Right now, I have a few loose ends: a bit of unfinished business. My lawyer said there might be some loopholes, but he is taking care of everything. Right, brother dear!"

"Oh no," said Carol. "Didn't I tell you when those two put their heads together no one can get in their way, not even Mary," said Diana.

"Your lawyer is Brian."

"Yes, Nanny, I'm the family's lawyer. I'm underpaid, over-looked, and overthrown. So Nanny, I just work for my family," said Brian.

John was standing in the doorway dying laughing at Brian.

"So trustworthy," he said to Brian.

Kara was looking at her family. She walked into the kitchen. She was thinking to herself. "Today everyone is so happy, so cheerful, and everything is so easy going. Maybe this story has a happy ending. Today all of my family is rejoicing. They all seem to like Mr. Grant. He's fitting right in with the tribe. Now that was one big surprise. Finding out my son is getting married. Then, I was taken by surprise again to find out that my little girl is moving to France, but I guess that's not too much of a surprise. She's always in France more than she is home."

"Larry has said that I'm his woman twice already. I think it's about time we have a talk. We really need it. My mother and father are acting like they like the man. My son kind of surprised me since he was the main one doing all the complaining in the first place. I can't believe my eyes. That's Brian for you."

CHAPTER EIGHT

Her mother is calling Kara.

"Yes, mom?"

"Baby, will you bring in the coffee and the desserts?"

"Yes, mom. Lord I need to get it together. I'm so nervous. This man is touching every nerve cell in my body. I need a time out. Does everyone want coffee and dessert?" asked Kara.

"No, my love, could I have a glass of wine? The dinner was delicious and very delightful. You know something, Kara? I have been eating in restaurants so much I didn't know how much a good, home-cooked meal could be so tasteful. I'm glad you invited me over today," said Larry.

Mr. Blackwell begins to talk.

"Young man, what do you do for a living?"

"Well, sir, I manage a few banks that my father owns. He owns about a dozen banks. A few chains between Spain and here. My sweet parents decided to move here to take over a couple of banks here in the states. My parents have lived here for sometime, close to ten years, give or take. He said it was about time to return back to Spain. So one day, mom and he got up and moved back home. So I had to come to the states and takeover some of his banking businesses. Some overthrowing and vice versa. Samuel, I'm more like a trouble shooter. I have to take care of all the problems, headaches, and all the responsibilities."

"Mr. Samuel and Brian, I want you to know I think the world of your daughter and mother. She is my spring flower. I couldn't ask for another any better than Kara. I wouldn't hurt her for nothing in the world. That you can count on. I will always take good care of my woman. She's been hurt one time, that's one time too many," said Larry.

"Well, thank you, young man. Now I can't ask from you any more than that. If you take care of my baby, you are a good man," said

Mr. Samuel.

"Yes! That is nice. Mr. Grant, how did you meet my uncle and aunt?" asked Brian.

"Well, Brian, you could say by playing a little golf. I like the game very much. Every chance I get I play 9 to 18 holes. You know I was minding my own business when I noticed a man and his friend kept watching me. I kept my guard up because they kept on watching me. So when I couldn't stand them watching me any more I stopped playing the game and walked over to them. I asked them was there a problem or something else? The man replied and said, no. Then he invited me to have a drink with them. And that's the way our friendship began."

"I also met John on the golf course. I tell you the man is a great player of golf. I would have never believed he was that great in that sport. John played against a couple of us, and we all lost to him. Every since then we have all become friends."

"Somewhere along the way, Larry decided to move back to the states. He was making this his residence, a place to call home. So along came my sweet wife and your aunt. She had been informed about Larry. Right away, she decided to poke her nose into somebody else's affair. We already know that she can't keep her nose out of somebody else's business. My wife's brain went into working overtime trying to think how she was going to put these two people together. She called your mother told her a good friend of the family was coming to town for a few days, and she would like for her to meet him. She also said that she was preparing dinner for their guest and wants her to come, also. Immediately, your mother's answer was no! She didn't need to meet any friend of the Nicholas family. She said it with so much anger and hostility that my wife's feelings were very much hurt. My wife became very emotional. She cried and cried. Finally I told her to keep out of people's business. But did she listen to me? No. If she had, she wouldn't be in this mess, walking around here weeping all day. So when she wouldn't stop crying, and I couldn't stand to see her so hurt anymore, I decided to take over the matter myself. I needed to get the true understanding of this problem. It was getting difficult at home. I had to help my wife and my sister, also. The three girls never said no to one another. Hell, we can be in bed, and my wife will get out of bed and go running to Kara or Pam when they call. That's how close the three of them are. The men in their lives don't mean a thing to them when it comes right down to those 'Jersey Girls.' Now that's how it goes with them. You'll see. So Larry, take a good look at those three women now because they are always going to have each others' backs. When Ronald and I said I do, he said I do to the three women, not just one."

"So, I knew I had to get to the bottom of this. Then, Carol called and said her mother was walking around with a long face, too. I knew then it was time for me to make my house call. I went to your mother's house, and we had a long talk. The rest, we all know," said Willie.

"My wife was so mad because she didn't find out until a week ago. Ms. Thang came into the shop to get some things, and that's how she found out about the man. She and my wife have made up, and now we are all here today. Thanks to the Lord because I can't take it when my wife gets upset. She's a walking time bomb. And please don't let anything happen to the children," said Ronald.

"Okay, Uncle Willie, is that really how my mother met her man?" questioned Carol.

"Yes, sweetheart, it really is," replied Uncle Willie.

"Wow! And what a man! Mother you sure found Mr. Right," said Carol smiling.

"Mr. Willie, I understand when you decide to speak, everybody stops and listens. We sure know one person that will never cross your path again. We understand that your talking can be hazardous to one's health. It can be a risky condition to your mind, body, or even cause a heart failure."

"Baby, we have all had a good time talking about the good old days. Are you leaving for the island next week? You have a good time. You sure need this trip. And Helen I understand you are going to take care of everything."

"That's a good man you have found. I will see you before you leave for the trip – right?"

"Yes, mother. Everything was just a delight today. The breakfast and the dinner was just great. Brian and Mary keep up the good work and take care of that sweet little baby."

"Yes Mom-mom. Oh, Mom-mom, we love you."

"That's so sweet," answered Nanna.

"Brian, bring the baby over to the house tomorrow. I brought something back for you," said Nanna.

"What time would you like for me to come by?" asked Brian.

"Well son, I'll say about noontime. Your Papa should be up by that time."

"Family, it's about that time. It's been a long day, and I need my rest. Your mother and I are going to leave now. Kara, I will see you tomorrow. I need to talk with you about some things. Come by when Brian and the kids leave. Make sure you call first."

"Okay daddy," answered Kara.

"John are you taking us home?"

"Yes, Papa. Wait father and mother, we are so glad you're back home. We have missed you."

"Father, can we come over next Sunday and have a cookout at home? We will bring everything over that you need. And daddy, we know you like to Bar-be-Que on the grill, but it's not just for you. Daddy, we want to give Kara and Larry a nice send-off on Sunday," said Pam.

"That's so sweet. Of course, you can have a cookout at home. I would love for you to have a cookout. Your mother and I have been on the go so much that we haven't had time for a bar-be-que. That's sounds real good baby. I'll love to help out. What time, child?"

"Well little lady, what time do you think? This time there will be no staying in the bed all day."

"How about 11 a.m. after you and mother are up? But mother you won't have anything to do. We will take care of everything."

"Who has to work on Saturday?"

"I only know two people that works on Saturday, and that's Willie and me. But this time we will take the day off," said Pam.

"Baby, you might be on call that day. If I am, I'll keep my beeper on. That way I can be here with my mother. She will be out of my eyesight for two long weeks," said John.

"Well Dad, everything has been taken care of for Saturday. Kara and Larry, we will see you two next Saturday at daddy's house," said Pam.

"Carol, we haven't been asked to do anything. Mom just said we should be at the house. So, Carol, you can't go to France this time. Mom is putting her feet down on this one. She's running this show."

"Yeah! And you can't hideaway in your little secret hideaway – the mystery place."

"Okay you two."

Diane and Carol looked at each other and started laughing.

"John, I love you. Mom, I'm so happy for you, and we will talk. So keep it until we have a chance to talk. I need you to have a good time."

"Night, Mom," said John.

"I love you, too, son. Good night to you. Lillian, it was so nice to meet you. Welcome to the family."

"Thank you, Mrs. Baker," said Lillian.

Lillian gave Mrs. Baker a hug, and Mrs. Baker hugged her back.

"Good night, my child," said Kara.

John and all walked out the door saying their good-byes to the family. Brian and his family were also saying good night.

"Mother, I'm sorry the way I was acting before towards Larry, but you have to be sure about people today. Mom, I sure don't want you hurt anymore by any man. If this man doesn't treat you right he has me to talk to. Mom, I love you. Do have a nice time. Good night mom."

"Good night, baby, good night my sweet little angel, good night Mary. Take care of my sweet, little angel."

"Yes mother, good night."

"We all love you, Nanny."

"I love you, too."

Pam and Helen were hugging and kissing Kara.

"We still are the 'Three Jersey Girls.' You just remember that, and we love you. You take care of yourself and be happy. Also be a little careful and do take your time before rushing into something without carefully thinking it through," said Pam.

"Okay you two, I love you, too. Let's have lunch before I take this trip so we can all talk at one time."

"Yeah right."

All three started to laugh. Then, they were all shedding tears. Willie come and get your wife and stop the crying," said Kara. "Good night, Helen. Ronald come and get your wife. Good night to all," said Kara.

Everyone walked out the door. Larry closed the door with his arms around Kara's waist.

"I need you, my love. Why did you keep on giving me dirty looks? Without any doubt, you could have taken my head off today. Baby, I meant every word I said to your family. Look here woman, you are mine."

Larry was laughing. Kara was getting mighty hot. This man was like a lion ready to attack the enemy.

"Come on my love, and have a glass of wine with me. Baby we have one week before we go on this trip to the island. You know something, I like your family. They are all very nice. Your daughter is okay, too. You're right, Carol is all for herself. Now I can help her with her school if she needs some help. Tell her to call me on Thursday. I have to fly out on Monday to Spain. I need to see my parents. Diane looked right at me as if she was reading every word I said. I don't think she likes me very well. Oh yes, your Ms. Pam told me if I hurt one hair on your head, my ass was grass, and she was the lawnmower. Brian and John were standing right beside me when she said it. Your two sons just laughed at me. Brian said, "Right-on, mom-Pam." Then she walked right out of the room. Diana heard her, also, and she was laughing, too. She was actually shedding tears. Nanny was so funny. She looked at me with a smile on her face. I know she could like me. I know by the way she was acting. But overall your family is very nice."

"Your son, Brian, turned out to be the law. I was having so much trouble with him. He is a damn good lawyer, but I still won the case by a thin line. Baby when I walked into your house and saw that man, I said, "Oh, no! Not him." Baby, I knew right away I was going to have some trouble with him. But he turned out to be very nice."

"Your father reminds me of my father. Your mother runs the show to a point, but your father lets her know who is the boss," said Larry.

"Oh my, God, Larry! How did you know that?" asked Kara.

"Didn't I just say your father is like my father in so many ways? He's still the boss in every routine. Kara, I'm going to say my good-nights until next week because I'm going to Spain to see my parents and to take care of some small business. I'll call you everyday, my love, until I get back. Then he takes Kara in his arms and gives her a long kiss. I want you to try and remember who really cares for you, my love. Good night, my little spring flower."

Larry walks out of the door and didn't look back. Kara closes the door with tears in her eyes. For about fifteen minutes, she just stands and thinks about Larry. "Today turned out to be a good day. No one acted up. Father was here, so he kept everyone in line. I haven't told anyone I'm not ready to go on this trip, not right now. It is too late, and I sure as hell don't want Willie on my back, not again. One time was enough for her that's for sure."

She needs to tidy up the kitchen, but instead she walks into her bedroom. She was tired. She was going to take a shower and head for the bed. She needs some sleep. She had some paperwork to take care of. There's a knock at the door. In walks Carol.

"Mom!"

"Yes, baby?"

"I really had a nice time this evening. You know, mom, everything went very well and to see Papa and Nana, it was so good to see them back at home. Mom, Mr. Larry is something else. When did you become his woman? Wow! My woman, the words just kept running out of his mouth like water running off a duck's back."

"Okay, Carol," said Kara.

"But mom, he kept on saying it. As if he was trying to make sure everybody knows that you belong to him. Diane was looking at him as if she didn't care for him, but she didn't say too much one way or another. But trust and believe, Mom Pam told him what she would do to him if he hurts you. All of us were laughing at him," including Diane.

"I know baby. He told me what your Mom Pam had said. He also said all my children were laughing, but he's alright with everything. Carol, he mentioned to me about your school. He wants you to know if you need some help, he would be glad to give you a helping hand. And if you feel you need help give him a call. Would you like to tell me why you are home tonight? It's still early. What? No going out for you tonight," asked Kara?

"No mom, I'm staying home tonight. I need to get up early tomorrow morning. I have two new models coming to class, so I need my rest. Remember, I just returned from France this morning. I still need more rest. Mom Pam also needs me to come over to the store. She needs to start on her inventory. She needs a helping hand tomorrow."

"Mother, you did say Larry said he would help me out, right? That is so nice of him. I'll ask Brian and Uncle Willie to talk to him. Good night mother," said Carol.

"Good night, baby."

Kara had been working so hard that morning. She was trying to get everything in order before leaving for the two week vacation. She had to bear in mind this is the first time she has ever closed her door. She has never been away from her agency since the day she opened up. Nevertheless, she hasn't been out of the states since she's been married and started her family. Once the children came along she didn't need to go away. She was happy just being a wife and a mother. Every now and then she would take the children on a weekend trip. Now here she is about to take a vacation based on what her friend, Helen, was talking about. She needs to live a little, yes, a little on the crazy side.

Taking a trip to the Virgin Islands with a man! And a man she doesn't really know too much about! And taking a leave of absence from her job for two weeks. She had been trying to come up with all kinds of excuses. She was thinking about what Larry had told her one day. He had mentioned to her he would make her darkness shine, and she needs to step right out into some sunlight. So her able body has already said yes to him, and there's no turning around now. It's a little bit too late now. No more excuses, just go on until the end.

"Well, Ms. Kara, you only have four more days before boarding the big ship. Old girl, you need to get your act together and start closing up loose ends. Make sure Jenny gets all the new contracts and letters out before you leave. You will be on your way out Sunday morning. I need Jenny to do some last minute packages. They need to be in the mail today."

Kara picks up the phone and calls Jenny to come to her office.

"Yes, Kara," said Jenny.

"Jenny, I need you to take some notes. There are a few more letters and packages that need to go out today. Jenny will you and your friend be going away on your two week vacation," asked Kara?

"No, Kara. I will be staying at home. My friend is going away with his family for a week. He won't be around to bother me. So all I plan to do is look at some good movies and have a few drinks of wine. I'm going to take it easy for one beautiful week without a living soul in sight."

"Well that sounds good to me. I will be leaving the office around noon, and I will not be coming back today. Jenny as soon as you finish with the letters and packages, you may close and lock everything up, and you may have the remainder of the day off. I still need two things from you. First make two phone calls. Please call Mrs. Nicholas and Mrs. Brown. Tell the two ladies to meet me at Tom's Bar and Grill at 12:30 p.m. The last thing I need you to do is collect the mail. If you think something is important and needs some attention, please call John or Brian. They will come by and pick it up. Your paycheck is in my desk. I also paid you for the two weeks vacation and for the remainder of today. Have a good time on your days off. I will talk to you before I leave. I will be here until Sunday morning."

"Kara, I don't think I will be needing you for anything, but if I do, I will call you. You go and have a good time with that handsome man of yours. He is something to look at. A man like that could take me to the end of the world and back again. Kara, isn't that the greatest gift you have ever received? That is the most valuable gift. It must bring you lots of happiness and fills a real need in your life. It sure has brought great value to you personally," said Jenny.

"My, God, Jenny, that was so sweet to hear you say that. You're trying to make me feel so bad. I do appreciate this trip, and I'm happy about it and a little on the sad side, too. But I will be alright. Jenny, I'm leaving now so I can get there about the same time the ladies walk into Tom's Bar and Grill," said Kara.

"Okay, have a good time today. The ladies said they will meet you. I will take care of everything here, and Bon Voyage to you," said Jenny.

Kara walked out of her office and got into her car. She drove off toward Tom's Bar and Grill. Without any problems at all, she arrived at Tom's. Her two friends were already there at the bar standing outside talking to each other. Kara parked the car and walked up to Helen and

Pam.

"Hello, ladies, it's hugging and kissing time."

All three had a group hug. The three started to laugh.

"Yeah, right, Ms. Thang, I need a drink, so let's walk into the bar and get it on. Helen we need to talk to Ms. Thang before she sails away from us."

"Yeah, you're right, Pam. We need that drink. Thank you, Kara, for calling this meeting at Tom's Bar and Grill. Still at the restaurant, the three ladies walked in the bar and right to the back of the bar where all the tables were. Hey! Let's get a table away from other people."

"Oh no! Look Kara this is the same corner table we were sitting at the last time we were here."

"Kara, what's up with this gathering today?"

" I need to talk," said Kara.

"Good, I also could use some time of sanity. Well, Ms. Thang, we could all talk about your trip, and I need a drink, too," said Pam. "What are we drinking today?"

"Hello Ladies, it is so good to have you back. It is indeed a pleasure to have you back again. It's been a very long time since I've seen you nice ladies. Would you ladies like to have your special drink?" asked Bob.

"Well, hello, Bob. Are you telling us you remember us and remember our drink?"

"Bob, will you be so nice and tell us about our special drink," said Helen.

"Okay, ladies. Your special drink was the Daiquiri. I also remember Kara was crying buckets of tears. She was crying and drinking. She had five Daiquiris."

"Oh, come on, now. Bob you're telling us you can remember that far back. That was some time ago. At least three years ago. That was the time I had a strong dislike toward a person. I formed a hatred thing that day," said Kara.

"You three ladies lit up the place. Who wouldn't remember you ladies? Your drinks are coming right up," says Bob.

"Ms. Thang, are you ready to take this fantasy cruise?" asked Pam.

"Yes and no," stated Kara.

"Alright, Ms. Thang, let's have it – the yes and no thing. My friend, you're not going to use that line about I can't go because my children need me are you? That certainly is not going to work this time. Our children are all grown-up. They are all young men and ladies now.

So, that one will not go over too well. Also, the little one has a sweet mother. So that's a no-no, too. So let's have it, Ms. Kara," said Helen.

"So Ms. Thang you need to start explaining to us right now," said Pam.

You know, it's like this. My yes is I'm ready to go but not really. I really don't have any excuses this time. I appreciate him wanting to take me on this cruise. I am ready. I closed my office today, and took care of everything on that end. And my no is, well, I'm a little on the nervous side, but I'll be okay by Sunday morning. Helen, you and Pam act like I can't do anything without my babies."

She was laughing.

"Now come on you two. Those are still my babies. They still need their mother at times," said Kara. "Look at it this way. You guys need an answer. Well, I will try to give you something just to make you two happy. You're right. They still need us all at times. So, let's get on with the trip.

"We don't need you to start changing your mind at the last minute. Now do we?" said Helen.

"Alright, give it a break okay, Helen? Ms. Thang, is Mr. Right back from Spain?" asked Pam.

"Yes, Pam. He came back this morning. He called to tell me he would see me tonight. And we are not going to any restaurant. He needs a good home cooked meal."

"So, ladies, am I being a little pushover if I should cook this meal for him tonight? Am I doing the right thing or the wrong thing? I'm talking about cooking for Larry. I don't want him to think I'm trying to get close to him by cooking. I need some advice, an answer now. Ladies, I need an answer today not tomorrow, okay?" said Kara.

"Look at it this way. You have already cooked for the man before. He did run out and tell everybody he likes your cooking. All I can say is to cook for him. He's a good man. His friendship to us is completely trustworthy. I, myself, have faith in him. Now that's my feelings about him," said Helen.

"Yeah! I cooked for everybody that day, not just for him." said Kara.

"Yes, Ms. Thang. You're right. Everybody was over on that day. No one ever said my woman or the food was so good like he was. So shut the hell up, Kara. I would cook this man one nice meal, candlelight dinner with the whole works. Meeting him at the door with a glass of wine. Have on one of the sexiest black gowns I could find with a big smile on my face. Larry likes wine. You already know what he likes, so go for it!" pronounced Pam!

"Oh, hell no! Pam would walk to the door butt-ass naked with a big-ass smile. The three were laughing and crying at the same time.

"Come on you two, stop it. You know I had no sex activity in six years or more give or take. You two know for a fact if I came on to Larry, he might think I'm a little on the crazy side. So ladies, no thank you. I'm not ready for that right now, anyway," says Kara.

"Look here, Kara, Larry would look at you with a big-ass smile on his face and say, "Baby, am I getting my dessert before the main course. Hell, woman, he'll just pick you up and nicely carry you into the bedroom and make some mad, strong, passionate love to you," says Pam.

"My God, Pam, I can't believe you're talking to me like that."

"Like what, Kara? You act like that damn asshole Mike just up and took your sexual desire life with him. Get a life, Kara."

"Alright now, Pam, put a hold on it. Give the girls a break. You telling us you still meet Mr. Ronald at the door with a glass of wine?" asked Helen

"Yes, Mrs. Helen, I do have to keep my man happy the best way I can. Sometimes I meet him with a glass of champagne and, like you said, without any clothes on, too. He is always so cheerful. In the mornings, he is rejoicing. We both have a very high spirit toward one another."

"Look, Kara, I don't mean to hurt your feelings, but you've been hurt one time by that no good husband of yours. Kara, don't get me wrong. You know the four of us have always had your back from day one. I have to give credit to him. He deserves credit for being a damn good father. His children never went without, that's for sure. He's always been only a phone call away from his children. But he's a hellava' poor husband to you. That's all everybody wants for you is to find a good man. That's what Helen and I want for you. A man that loves you and only you. Larry is the man for you, Kara. He really cares for you. Ronald and I were talking about you and Larry the other night. Ronald said he likes the man. They were at the golf course the other day, and he was talking to him. He likes the way the man was talking. Think now. You know my husband doesn't like too many people."

"Kara, I like Larry. I think he's the right man for you," said Pam.

"Not you Mrs. Pam Brown. I've been telling you along he's a good person. He's the right man for Ms. Thang. He is Mr. Right. She will never find another man like Larry Grant. That's for sure. She better catch him. He's a person worth catching and fastening on to. Hold on to him. He'll make you a damn good husband. You need to make a start. First, by getting better acquainted with him. Next, let him be the one to break the iceberg. He shouldn't be calling you an ice cold woman," says Helen.

"If Ms. Thang will do as we tell her, she'll be a hot ass mom cooking for her hot dad."

Both ladies were laughing hard at Kara.

"Okay ladies, be nice for a change. First you want me to walk to the door butt-naked. Now you're talking about catching a husband and something about an ice woman. What's next you two?" asked Kara.

"Kara, we are trying very hard to be a little nice, but this Daiquiri is making me a hot momma. I need Willie to be at home so he can take care of his hot momma," said Helen.

"Oh Bob! Will you keep bringing the Daiquiris for the three 'Jersey Girls?'

"Yes, I'll bring them for the crying girl, the giggling girl, and the laughing girl, too. Do I need to bring out the bucket for your tears?" he asked. "I might need three buckets. Looks to me like you have all been crying and weeping. You all are the happiest women, even the crying woman. I have never seen three beautiful women cry so much as you ladies do," says Bob.

"You're right, Bob. That's the same thing our nice husbands say, too. So keep on putting the Daiquiris on the table. And Bob would you be so nice and call my son, John? Tell him to come and get his mothers, I'll say, in about a couple of hours because we sure can't make it home driving. We are in no shape to take ourselves home. Tell John, we are going to need three drivers. No one can move a car this day. This is my cell phone number, 371-6489. Thank you so much, Bob," said Kara.

"Kara, listen to us real good. Mr. Larry Grant is crazy about you. That's all he talks about. My woman this and my woman that. Hell! Anybody can see he really cares for you. He couldn't even take his eyes off of you. He was watching every move you made. Now he's taking you away in four more days on a cruise. Kara, he's knocking on your door. It's about time you open up that door and let him in. He's taking you to the Virgin Island. You go for it and don't look back," said Helen.

"You two are trying to make me a hot momma. I'm already acting like some crazy-ass teenager as it is. Hell, I'm getting so nervous at times. He's always saying ain't no shame in his game."

"Kara, I heard that ex-husband of yours called you the other day asking you about you and Larry. And what is this you going away for two weeks with a man you don't even know a thing about? Ronald was mad as hell with Mike."

"Pam, how did you know Mike called me? I didn't say a word to anybody about him calling me."

"Carol was home. She told you," said Kara.

"Yes, she did. She called her Papa and told him Mike had called you and said you were very upset," said Pam.

"You're right. She called you, too. Right Helen? Yes, Kara, and Willie called Mike and told him to leave you the hell alone. Or he would take the next step in his hands. Old Mike hung up the phone. He didn't say one word to Willie," said Helen.

"I know Carol was looking at me and asked was I alright before she left the house. I know Mike is a stone jackass. He's still trying to keep up with me, but it won't work. Not this time. Not any more. So now you two are telling me what to do. I still think I'm a big girl now. I think so, but let me have it," said Kara.

"Well, you do know that Larry told Father he was a trouble shooter. Kara that man could shoot all kinds of trouble in your bed. He could have you crying out for more. He could shoot a hole right in your soul."

"You two should play a little bank game. He comes along and put his love into your bank, girl. You'll be calling my Larry, come back baby, put some more and more. Oh Larry, shoot it to me, baby. Shoot it to momma. I need it. You're the best there ever was," said Helen.

Kara and Pam were laughing and crying out, "My God!"

"Helen, we'll be playing bank? He put his love in my bank? How did you come up with that? I have always said you were crazy as hell," said Kara.

"You're right. That's why Willie has to make sure he keeps his license. He needs the authority to put you away," said Pam. "You are crazy as hell. You talking as if I need some action before I take this cruise, saying I need a booty call. You, too, Mrs. Pam. Today you are telling me you like Larry. I'm glad because a few days ago you were telling Larry you were going to mow his ass. You two are crazy as hell. You two still saying you have my back. I don't think so. You two fools are trying to put me in bed with Larry," said Kara.

"Oh, hell, Mrs. Thang. How do you know I was going to mow his ass," says Pam

"Because he told me so," say Kara.

"My God, Pam, you were going to do what to him?"

She was laughing at Pam and Kara.

"Look, Helen, you know the man and do you remember I just

met the man last Sunday. I didn't know anything about him. So I was making sure he didn't hurt Kara. So I nicely told him if he hurt one hair on her head his ass was grass and I was the lawn-mower," said Pam.

"Damn. You're one bad-ass woman, Pam."

Helen was laughing so hard she had tears running down her face. Then all three were laughing.

"You know something, Pam. I am going to tell Willie this. He wouldn't believe you said that to his friend, Larry."

"Yeah right! You and your big mouth."

"Look here, Kara. I am real sorry about that but more for what I said to Larry. My children were in the room. They heard me say that to Larry. Diane was looking at Larry and me with that delightful look on her face. But she did not say a word. Just look and smiled," said Pam.

"Oh, that's alright. Larry is a big boy. He will get over it. He can take care of himself. But now you two little hell-cats are coming home with me and help cook your Mr. Right a good home-cooked meal this evening. After you hell-cats finish helping me, then, ladies, you're going home to your nice husbands."

"Hell, we are intoxicated and too emotional right now. We need to stop drinking," said Kara.

"You're right, Ms. Thang. Let's have one more for the road. Boy! I've always wanted to say one for the road," said Pam. "Kara about dinner, just give the man a light dinner. I'm giving Ronald a light dinner this evening. Light and quick gumbo chicken soup, tossed salad, baked potato, and a nice T-bone steak. That's good, and it's sure a home-cooked meal," said Pam.

"Hell yeah, Kara, that sounds good to me. He will love it, baby. Hell, it sounds so good Willie shall be eating the same thing. Thanks, Pam. You know I'm too wasted to cook a big meal tonight. I will love making Willie happy tonight – never mind," said Helen.

"Oh! So you hell-cats are telling me it's a no-no. You're so right."

"Wait a minute. We will go with you home this evening and set up your dining room. We will also help you with the meal. Put on some soft music, and we know he likes wine. Do you have any wine at home? If not, we will pick up some. We have to go to the supermarket to get our own dinner and yours, too, Kara. Larry likes the Bordeaux Red Wine."

"Ms. Thang, our men, will have the same meal with candle light – the whole works tonight. So, you see, we still have your back Ms. Thang," said Helen.

"You two are still running the show, having your way with me again. Right girls! You two have always been like this ever since we were children, and you're still doing it today."

"We love you, Kara," said Pam and Helen. "Hell, our husbands love you, too. Sometimes we think they love you more than they love us. Both men run to your every call. Pam, we have to make sure Larry Grant loves her and take her the hell away like to Spain."

"Hey Helen, can't you see Ms. Thang in Spain all by herself without any children."

"My children will not be leaving me!"

"My ass! She'll be on the phone calling."

"You're right. Our husbands to the rescue, again. Never mind. You just stay home with us. We still love you."

Pam and Helen were looking at Kara giggling.

CHAPTER NINE

"We got you, Ms. Thang. Don't try and push our buttons," said Pam. "So, Kara, Sunday you will be flying out to Florida to take your ship to the Virgin Island. One week you guys will be in the Virgin Islands, and the next week you will be on the ship sailing around the other Island," say Helen.

"Yes, that is what Larry said we will be doing.

"Oh no, Pam, this is all wrong we all should be on that ship with you Kara. We three never been without the other some where around. You will miss us, Kara, and stop that crying.

"Hell, that's why he's taking her now so we could not go. Helen, the man wants her all to himself," says Pam.

"Oh, come on, you two, I'll be alright. That I promise you. I will call you all when I get to Florida and just before we get on the ship. And I will be seeing you all on Saturday at Daddy's house. Are you all going with me to the airport on Sunday?" asked Kara.

"No, Kara, that is too much. I can't see you going away without the three of us, or I will start crying. So we will all say our bon voyage on Saturday, old girl."

"Well, hello, mothers. You all are drunk. Mother, didn't you ladies eat anything today?"

"No, son, we were too busy talking and drinking to think about some food.

"Oh, John, thank you for coming. Your three mothers needed an evening to ourselves before Kara takes this here vacation. We need some time away for the family. Saturday everybody will be at Pop-pop's house. Thank you. You brought Carol and your Lillian. Thank you for coming to get your mom's. Yes, all three mothers really need to go home now."

"How many drinks did you ladies have?" asked John?

"We were not counting. We drank and talked and cried," said Helen.

"Well, let's go home. Oh, wait one minute. We are all going to your mother's house to help her with her dinner and set up her dining room table for her," said Helen.

"Mom Helen, my mother does not need help in her kitchen," says Carol.

"Oh, yes, she does this evening. She is cooking a special meal for her Mr. Larry. We all need to try catching this here man for our Kara," said Pam.

"Oh, mother when did Mr. Larry get back home?" asked Carol.

"This morning, baby," said Kara.

"Well, I need to talk to him about our school," said Carol.

"Well, little one, I think you will have to do your talking on the phone tonight because I need to talk to you. So come by the house. We need to talk before you go back to Paris, baby. So you can have dinner with me and Ronald, if that's alright with you, baby," said Pam.

"Oh, yes, Mom Pam, I also need pop Dad (Ronald) to do me a cup of favor," said Carol.

"Hello, did all our moms pay up your tab?" say John.

"Yes we paid up," said Kara.

"Well, can't we all leave this here place, mother, before you ladies get another drink for the road? My, if the husbands could see you two ladies, there would be some mad men. My mother, your Brian and Mrs. Diane would need forgiving. You, my mother, do no wrong to her. Your baby would not be happy about this, my mother. I am not too happy, so let's go home," said John.

"You look here, Mr. Smarty Pants, why do you think we called for you. We thought that you would come for us, and here you are getting an attitude with us, but we all love you, John and Carol. You two need to close your mouths or your mother will stop all that gift money. You're still a young intern trying to climb up that ladder. You, too, Ms. Carol. You, too, are climbing up that ladder of success. The other two are already up that ladder. We love you both," says Pam.

"Lillian you take a good look at this here family because I am going to welcome you to our little, crazy family. I want you to meet the three 'Jersey Girls.' You have seen one, but the other two are standing. Look over your left shoulder. You can believe me when I tell you. The 'Jersey Girls,' now, they travel in pairs, so, Lillian, I heed you to listen to me real good now. You said you love me, right? Well, if you really love me, I will gladly welcome you too this here family. You see those three little ladies are my heart. They come with this package, so, my Lillian, do be aware if you choose me that you need to make sure that you go all the way. So, I think you need to give it some thought. If you think you can hang in there, then you come right on in with the rest of the crazy family. My mothers, they cry, they laugh, and also giggle. But we all love them to death. They will always have my back. So, if you don't choose us, you can return your package. It is as simple as that," said John.

"Well my son, we thank you so very much for those sweet, wonderful words, and you are just nice and welcome, Lillian, to the family. But your little family is not that crazy. We just like to have a good time."

"Yes, but not that crazy, not yet anyway," say Kara.

"Yes, we all love you, John. So now let's go to the supermarket. We still need to do some shopping. We need food and some wine for Larry. So let's go now," said Pam.

"Oh, hell no, you are not going to no store. Not this day. We are going to take you three mothers home, and put you three ladies to bed before your boss comes home and finds you two ladies like this. And my mother, stop that crying, please. John, you take your mother home and put her in bed. She needs to get some rest before Larry sees her. We don't need him to see her this way. He might never come back. We try to distract him. So you make sure she is laying down and then lock up. And John, you go and pick up Lillian at mom Helen's house, and I'll be over. We will go to the store together. So you wait for me at mom Helen's house. That way we won't have to take but one car."

"Now Lillian, by the way, you are welcome to the family now. This is the time to see if you can hang. Now, mom Helen is your job. You will take her home. She just lives a block over from mother's house. Mom Helen can tell you the right one, and Lillian don't let her give you a hard time. If so, call me. You also need to make sure she is lying down. John will be coming over to lock up. Now, I will take my mom Pam home and put her in bed, too. John, you make sure my mother is all right before you leave that house. And that goes also for you too, Lillian. You ladies need some rest before you think about cooking tonight. So you ladies give us your list of items you need for this here dinner tonight. We three will be going to the store to do the shopping. So give me some money now."

"Let's go home right now. No more talk," said Carol.

"Oh, man, is that my baby Carol talking like that? Hell, who died and left her in charge of our life? You better get your bag, money, and list out, or she might just make us go to bed without any food tonight. Hell, she might just tell her daddy on us."

The three ladies get up, walk to the door, and stop to say bye to Bob. They walk out of the bar just laughing, saying we look like we are the little children right now.

Bob said, "Night ladies, come again. And thank you all," but the ladies did not hear him.

Each woman got in the car that Carol had said. They all left Tom's Bar and Grill.

Early Saturday morning, Kara and her girl were up early trying to get every thing ready for the cook out.

"Mother, you are not making your child breakfast this morning? I hope you know that your child is very hungry," said Diana.

"Yes, my baby, your mother has to go to your Pop-pop's house to cook breakfast this morning for everybody. So, my little girl, you might have to find yourself something to eat in the refrigerator to hold you over until this old lady can get to the house and start to cook. I love you, too, my little girl."

"My father, he called me the first thing this morning to tell me to come to the house and cook for everyone. He would like to feed everybody. That way you will be at daddy's house all day after breakfast. He will start on the cook out. That way he will have everybody at the house. He likes to put every live soul to work. My father gets a kick out of it."

"So, my child, as you said, that is why your mother is not cooking at home. Also, that is the reason we are taking all this food for breakfast and the cookout food, everything to your Pop-pop's house. Your mom Helen and her family are already at the house. Oh, can you guess who is home this week?"

"No, mom."

"Well, your two little cousins are home. Helen and Willie are so happy this morning. George and Crystal came home last night. I would love to see them. It has been a very long time. It's been almost one year since I saw the two children. It is almost that time for them to be getting out of college by now. Helen will soon have two more doctors in the house. She is very happy about it. Oh, yes, your uncle Timothy and his family are all coming over this time so Helen and Mary are there to help mother out. John said he was going to bring Lillian over before he goes to the golf course."

"The men are going to play a few games of golf this morning, so they won't be in anyone's way. That is the excuse they are trying to use so they don't have to work. When they come back, all the food will be ready to eat. Your mom Pam called and said she is on her way over here to take some of the food to the house. She also has some food to take to the house," say Kara.

"Oh, mother, did you make the potato salad and the bean

salad?" asks Diana.

"Yes I did. I also need you to cut up the vegetables for the tossed salad. And girls, do put everything in the bowl that's on the table for me please. We also need to wash all the meat and put it in the big bowl. Also, when Pam gets here, we can start putting food in my car and her car. Oh, yes, Carol, Larry said he will talk to you and Brian today about your school," said Kara.

"Thank you, mother, for asking Mr. Larry. I will be sure that Mr. Lawman knows about it," said Carol.

"Good morning, everybody. Is everyone about ready to go?"

"Yes, mom Pam. And how is my mom Pam this here morning?"

"Well, baby, your mom is doing just fine. How are you this morning, Kara?"

"Just fine, Pam. Oh, my, Diana, you look so tired this morning, baby. How do you feel? You wouldn't be sick would you baby?" asked Pam.?

"Oh no, my mom, Pam, your child is just tired and needs her rest. You know today is my rest day. I need all the rest I can get now days. Now, my mother knows this is a no-no day, but my two mothers have me out here for a good, old cook out."

"I could be in my bed getting me some good old rest," said Diana.

"Carol."

"Yes mother?"

"Carol, when are you going back to France?" asked Kara.

"Oh, mother, thank you for asking. You know, I forgot to get you to book me on a flight out of here. I need to be back in Paris by 8:00 p.m. Friday night. I have to do some modeling. So mother, you know I forget you were leaving on Sunday morning on your trip. Can you still book me on a flight before you leave? For your, baby," said Carol.

"Oh yes, my child, you do not need to worry your little head off. Your mother has your back. I will book you on a plane right now," said Kara.

She walked into her home office.

"Mom Pam, I'll be back in Paris for a week, and I need to do some shopping for you. The new model lines are out and all new stock will come in next week. So, I will do some shopping for you," said Carol.

"Well, my two young ladies, you will be flying out of here at 6:00 p.m., Friday morning, first class. So, Ms. Diana, you will be going to Paris with your sister, Carol, for two whole weeks. You need a nice vacation. So your mother is sending you away. No excuses," said Kara.

"Look mother, I really do not need a vacation. Oh. Mom, you hurt my feeling. But that is alright because you opened the door to your heart now. You tell me to get up and do the same thing. But my sweet mother, neither love nor Mr. Right have I found, not yet anyway. So how about stop wasting your time telling me about my life. Why can't we just love one another and try to live together in a little peace," said Diana.

"My sweet, little Diana, your speech will not work this time. You will start getting on up and getting yourself a life. I do not need you to start following right in my foot steps."

"My God, Pam, talk to your spoiled child. You make things even worse by giving in to the spoiled-ass children. They have their way so much that they demand or expect it from you and Ronald or Mike. He comes right along and does the same thing. I never like spoiled-ass children. Do you three hear me? Diana, you are still going to Paris with Carol. You are your own boss when you get ready to close your door there is no obligation at all. And you have no kind of an excuse at all either way but to put your butt on that plain to Paris. Carol, you take care of your sister," say Kara.

"Oh, now, mother, I am not some little baby. But I well take this here trip. But, my God, mother, you call me a spoiled child. Well I hate to tell you, but you are right along the same road. You just bought me a ticket to go to Paris. So, who is the spoiled one now? You are doing the same thing, but you know something mother? I am so glad that you love me that much, to make sure that I am happy."

"I love you, too, mother. I will go to the big city, Paris, with Carol," say Diana.

"Oh, thank you, Diana, for going to Paris with me. You can help me out with some modeling. That's the week Lillian will be out in East of France. She will be taking care of new models that will be coming to the new school. So it can be like old times when we were in college. I'll take you shopping and do some sight seeing. We will visit lots of places and things that will be of some interest to you."

"We used to live in Paris and loved it, too. We had some good times, sister girl," said Carol.

"Come on you two. Let's go before daddy calls again to see what is the hold up. Who is riding with who?"

"I will ride with mom Pam," said Carol. "So let's go, Ms. Diana.

Everyone got in the cars to leave to go to Kara's father house.

"Well, it's about time you decided to come ladies. I am waiting for my breakfast very patiently, and the cook is no where to be found," said Mr. Samuel.

"Good morning, Pop-pop," said Diana, Carol, and Pam.

He was smiling.

"Well, morning to you too, my daughters. Well, well my little Carol is still at home. You have been running back and forth to France. And by the way, Ms. Carol Lee, why do you have to open up another modeling school and in a foreign country at that, like France? Anyway, couldn't you just open up another school right here in your own state? Yes sir, like I told that mother of yours about a hundred times, not to send you kids to no Paris to some modeling school. Oh no, she and Mike sent you kids anyway, just like we don't have no modeling schools right here in your own state."

"I guess not because your parents just up and packed you two kids off to Paris so you could get a better education. I did ask your mother could you kids learn the same thing here at home, but I guess not because you are now a specialist. Now you are a number one top model. You are a trainer and teacher. You help others. You are all about this modeling thing, and, baby, you are very good at it, too. Your old Pop-pop is so proud of all his grandchildren. Now all I need is some more grandchildren by you two girls. So when are you two young ladies getting married? You do know that you two are not getting any younger. So don't you think it is time you two start looking for Mr. Right?"

"I do, but also make sure now that he is the right man, and he is a man that work everyday that is all about taking care of a family. Not something like take care of him.

"We will not have that in this here family. Not at all. Everybody brings home the bread. We work together, side by side, in this here show, ok girls?"

"Yes, Pop-pop, but we need to find a man first that can take this here family."

"Pop-pop, the last one I was dating, he came home to meet the family, as you said. They took one look at him, John asked him to leave, and do not find his way back again. Pop-pop, can you remember that day. You know something, Pop. I liked him, too, Pop," said Carol.

"Well, baby, you will find that young man. One day he will come along and, believe me, John will not be able to send that one away this time. Okay, but baby that man was not for you anyway. That is why your brother sent him away. But, baby, in the future you will find Mr. Right," said Mr. Samuel. "Now, my Diana, it is your time, baby.

What are you doing with your life?"

"Well, Pop-pop, I am trying to make a good life right at home. I am working steady without giving up any patients. I do have too many right now. My staff is refusing to let anymore come in, and I hate to turn anyone away. But, Pop, I am over booking right now, and my boss is sending me on vacation for some two weeks in Paris with Carol. She thinks I stay at home too much, but Pop-pop, I have work up to my neck. I really do not have time for a love life. Not right now anyway. Mother bought my ticket already for me to take this trip. So I will go away for the two weeks. I just might need a rest for a few days, but Pop, I only have five days to take care of some of my patients before I leave."

"Pop, you know I love my mother, and I would never say no to her. Well, she is calling us. She said breakfast is ready," said Diana.

"You know something. You and Carol are some nice young ladies. You two never gave your mother any trouble. We all have spoiled you two. Now, I have two more grandchildren. Now my Helen's two are going to be doctors. My Brian's two just told me they are going to be. Wait, that was my little Michelle. She said she was going to be a doctor like her Pop-pop. She said she likes to have pretty teeth. That's my heart."

"She is running beside me," he laughed. "Now that Mark, he said that what he want to do is fly a jet plane all over the world. Not a lawman or a judge. He just wants to be that person who drops the bombs. He said that was so funny to him. It was amusing to him."

"He is too young to be talking like that," said Carol.

"I know that he is very young, but now days, it is so much mess on TV. Now days what can you expect for the kid. They can now learn knowledge and so much wisdom today. Now, your Nanny and me are so proud of all our children and grandchildren. They all turned out to be very wise and special to us."

"Now, I have three doctors, a judge, a lawman, and two teachers. Now that's good work. They are their own bosses."

"Pop-pop."

"Yes, child?"

"You have five doctors not three. You already had three before, but you did count the two that are coming into the family in about three more months," said Carol.

"Oh, well, thank you my child. Now when you get old like me, you forget things as things pass you by. Well, let's go in to eat breakfast. I asked your mother to cook for her old pop. I will not be here too much longer if that young man keeps on taking her off on the cruise ship."

"I will have to call on my other daughters to come and cook for old daddy. Your Nanny will not cook me fat food. Dianna, you are not looking too happy right now. Would you like to talk to your Pop-pop? Now I always have an open ear for you children. I didn't know you were to going on this here trip to Paris. If you do not want to go, you tell me, and I will tell that boss of yours you do not want to go. Now is that a yes? Or a no? You tell me right now."

"Oh no, Pop-pop, I am just a little on the tired side. That's all. Oh, I love to go. Mother is sending me away from home. Your little baby girl is going to fly right out of the nest."

She was laughing.

"Well, baby girl, that is a good way of looking at it. So you go and have a good time on your mother's money. Now child, you tell me am I right now. You said your mother is sending you back to Paris. Now you try to remember your last stay in Paris. For three weeks, you called home everyday crying to your Nanny that you was ready to come home. You said, "Nanny, I do not like it out here. You were crying so hard your Nanny took it in her hands and said to me, "Send her the money like she said" so you could come home. Now your mother and Mike was mad as hell. They said you could at last stay a month. Talk about the money they had lost on you. Now your mother was very upset with her mother because she did talk to her, and Mike she sent you the money."

"But your Nanny said, "Hell with you, Kara. My child, come home. So she came home. Now she is all grown up, so she will not be crying this time. You will not be using my money this time, that is for sure. So she is sending you again for two weeks," say Pop-pop.

"Oh, but Pop-pop, this will always be my home. I can't leave my mother and Nanny and mom Pam too long. All my family is right here. After all, I will miss talking to you about everything. You know they said the apple does not fall far from the tree. So I am not moving too far from my home. This little girl will not be too far for my loved ones if I need help.

"I like for you to be close by at all times. That way, you can come right away," said Diana.

"Well, here come the men. Well, now, everyone is here. So come on everybody, and let's have breakfast. Kara already called twice. So let us all head to the dining room to eat. Okay, everyone lets sit and bless the table. Baby, you always out do yourself when you cook. Young man, do you know you are taking my cook away from me? So, my other daughter, you need to start getting ready to cook for your father. Your mother will not ever think about cooking me fat food at all. Now, I do like a good home cooked breakfast every now and then. Like once a week. Is that not asking for too much? Just on special days and today is one."

"My baby will be leaving us. So, it's that time for my breakfast this morning because my child will be flying away from home with a man. This here family needs to get to know something about him. Yes sir, he's Mr. Right."

"Oh Daddy, why are you sure I will not be cooking for you no time soon. My God, father, I am only going away for two weeks. I am not moving away from home. This is my home. So why are you talking like that to me, father? Your daughter will always be at home," say Kara.

"Now, baby girl, you have a nice, young man. Now when he says let's go, you will be ready to go young lady because you will never find another Mr. Right like this here Larry Grant. My child, so you try to have a good time with this here young man, okay? Now Kara, you have two other sisters to take your place. My other girls already have their Mr. Right. They will be right here with us, right ladies?"

"Yes daddy."

"So, now, you just take care of your end. Right now your family wants you to live your life once again and a good life, too. Now that is all. Take care of my baby girl."

"Well, men, how was your morning on the golf course? I know you didn't let John win again this time."

"Oh, no, daddy it was John this time. It was the new comer, Mr. Brian. He is the new member. That's what he said, but he was playing like he has been at it everyday. Then, he's joining in with Larry. They paired off and left us three to play. Larry is good. So we just looked on and started teasing Larry about his woman, daddy," John said.

"Oh, Larry, my mother is cooking that special breakfast again. He was hurt because he didn't get breakfast the first time. So he was playing good, real good, too. We three had already lost our game. So, we decided that it was time to come home."

So we were walking back to the club house. The minute Larry heard that we were about to go home for Kara's breakfast, the man stopped playing golf, and he came running toward us. Daddy, he talked about his woman Kara," said Ronald.

"Look you guys. Kara didn't tell me anything about her cooking breakfast this morning. The only thing she said was your father was having a cookout sometime today. Now you guys are telling me that my woman is cooking a good, old-fashioned breakfast this morning.

Now the other time she cooked everybody breakfast, I was not invited to that one either, but this here one, I will be inviting myself to this one because you know something, Mr. Willie and Mr. John, I am so tired of hearing you two talk about my woman's cooking all the time. So like I just said, I will be attending this here one."

"I will certainly get me some breakfast this morning. I've been waiting a long time, so let's go now man. I need to see my baby anyway. I have started missing her already, so hell, you men get in the vehicle, and let's go home now," said Larry.

"Hell, I am starting to think my sister got the man hooked on her and also her cooking. Look men, do you think the man has it real bad, I mean really bad? But look here, Larry, don't feel bad. We're in the same boat you are in. So, you just come and go in the rest of the game. Now my sister can cook, but so can my wife can too, now," said Willie.

"Well, it's about time you men got back here. My baby was waiting on you men to eat."

"Yes, you're right. My baby is a very good cook. Also, you men now give Larry a break. The man has his own rule, and does not take any prisoners. But I have to tell you something, Larry. This here family does take a few prisoners because no woman in this here family will ever get hurt anymore by a man. My Kara was burned once, but that was one time too many. That so called ex-husband of hers. So what I am trying to tell you, Larry, is that will never happen again. That is why everyone is telling you not to hurt her. If you hurt her, you will have all the Blackwell family on your back. Now if you are for real, that is damn good. Now if you know I can't, I'm asking you very nice to start walking away right now. That way, your ass will be on safe ground away from any kind of damage. Now that ex-husband can tell you all about it. Larry, you did say that Willie is your best friend, right? Now you make sure that he is your friend at all times because, Larry, take it from this old man, sisters and wives we do not play with. Now your friend, Willie, was going to perform a nice, female test on Mike, your ex. My man was going to receive a free operation for himself by Willie that you do not need, right? So, Larry, I like you as long as you do not play around with my baby girl."

"Like we all said before, no one hurts our women folk. Now, Larry, look here man, let us start to play a little fair with Larry. Now he is taking my baby girl away for two weeks. Now lets us not frighten the man away. Now we're never going to catch him like this. He is a honest man. So let's not run him away before my baby gets her hand in the man's other hand. We sure do not need Ms. Thing mad with us or on

our ass now do we? Man, we sure do not want to be in the dog house.
Now that is for sure. You do not want to get that woman on your bad
side. She can be a hell raiser. You did say you were a trouble shooter.
You do like my baby girl, right young man?"

"Oh, yes sir, your daughter is a very important person in my
life. She is my spring flower, the princess of my life. You will never in
your life have to worry about me ever hurting your little baby girl. Sir, I
am a one woman man. I do not have but one lady-friend, and that is
your daughter. There had been a lot of talk about me being with a few
women, but someone told a lie. They also called me a womanizer, but I
am not. Your Kara is my princess from day one. Now if there's anyone
hurt, it will come from your daughter. She may run away from me.
She likes to stay locked up in a dark hole without light. I need her to
come out and see the world with me. That is why I am taking your
daughter on this here trip, to take her away from her hiding place
without looking back at her past but to the future."

"I know she has a long way to go to get things back in her life,
but if she will just let me hang in there then I think we may have some
kind of a future together. Mr. Blackwell, but that is left up to her. There
is nothing I would not do for her. She is a part of me, sir," said Larry.

"Well, thank you, young man. I can take my hat off to you.
Now, Mr. Larry has put us in our place, so now let's all go outside and
start the fire on this here cook out."

"I don't need my wife coming in here starting on me. You
know, Larry, we never really welcomed you to the family, but young
man, I, myself, am going to do that right now, but, first, I must ask do
all you man vote Larry Grant into this here family?"

"Yes, daddy, we all do."

"Well Mr. Grant, you are now welcomed to the Blackwell
family. You became a part of this here tribe. You were already welcomed by Kara. Now you are in with the rest of her tribe. But Larry,
when you become a part of this family, you take on the whole tribe.
You look out for everyone. We all stand together as one. We are a very
small family. I am the only child my parents had, and so is my wife.
She is the only one. We have two children. My son has only one child,
and you know the rest."

All the men walked outside to the patio. Mr. Blackwell walked
out to the backyard to start his grill up so he could begin his cooking
now. All the ladies were inside the house getting all the meat ready for
the grill and getting all the food ready for the cookout today. Little
Michelle came running outside to see her daddy, but instead she saw
Mr. Larry. She went running over to him. She asked Mr. Larry, "Why

did you make my Nanny cry, and also why are you taking my Nanny away from me and Mark? If you take her away, we will not have no more Nanny. My Nanny is crying because she is leaving me and Mark. My mother said you will be taking her away tomorrow morning, and I will not see my Nanny leave tomorrow with you, but my other Nanny said you will take good care of our Nanny. So now, Mr. Larry, you will be very careful with my Nanny, want you? Make sure you bring her back to us. Now I am mad with you, Mr. Larry."

If you do not bring her back, you will be so sorry because she will miss me and Mark, and she will be crying. You will have to bring her home or my mom and Nanny will be crying, too, and you no something, Mr. Larry? My mother and daddy will lock you up, and you be crying, too. I know I will be crying, so Mr. Larry, will you please bring my Nanny back home. We are her only grandchildren, me and Mark, and we need our Nanny. We love her so much. Okay, Mr. Larry?" said little Michelle.

"Oh, I am so sorrow little one. I promise you I will bring your Nanny back home to you and Mark. You know something little one? I will make sure your Nanny calls you every day. I will take very good care of your Nanny. She is very special to me, too. If she calls you, would that make you feel much better little one?"

"That way your mother and daddy will not have to look me up. How is that for a start, little one?" said Larry.

"Oh, yes, thank you, Mr. Larry. Now, I can tell all the ladies to stop crying now. See you, Mr. Larry."

"Hello, my Pop-pop, guess what just happened? Mr. Larry said he would take very good care of my Nanny. Now, she and all the other moms can stop all that crying. He said that he would bring her back home to us, Pop-pop. He also made me a promise to take real special care of our Nanny. You will also miss her, too, Pop-pop. We can't have anymore good breakfast if he does not bring her back to us, but he did say not to worry about her. Pop-pop, Mr. Larry said my Nanny was very special to him. Is that good, my Pop-pop?" said Little One.

"Yes, my child, that is very good. That means he cares for your Nanny, my child," said Mr. Blackwell.

"Oh, my Pop-pop, now I need to tell my Nanny she doesn't need to worry anymore. I have to take good care of my Nanny. She said I was her big little helper. So Pop-pop, I will be right back, and I need to talk to my daddy, too."

"But, my Pop-pop, can I help you cook on the grill, too? If I could cook like my Nanny, I could cook your good breakfast for you, my Pop-pop. So can I help you out today? But first, I need to talk to my daddy. I love you, my Pop-pop, see you. Hello, all my uncles gave me kisses and hugs, too. All my sweet uncles, I love you. My daddy, I love you, too. Can I have my kiss and hugs, daddy? Oh, my daddy, do you love me. All her uncles were laughing. She already knows how to get in a man's pocket. She will sweet talk you. She needs some money, so you uncles start getting your money out of your pocket. She said she loves you and kisses and hugs. That is our Little One," said John.

"Yes," said Brian. "Yes, my Little One."

"Good, my daddy. Your little one needs some money. I need to get my Nanny a going away present she needs something from me and Mark. That way she would know we gave it to her so she will be sure to come back home to us. And all my uncles, I need your money, too, to help me get a big present for our Nanny. I love her, daddy. That way she will remember to come back home. Also, daddy, I need you to take me to the store to get my Nanny a good present. You know something my daddy and my uncles, all the ladies are so busy in the kitchen crying over my Nanny. You know that my mom Pam said we all need to go with my Nanny. Then, they all started to cry all over against. My daddy, I asked my mother why she was crying. She said, Go and get your daddy. My mother needs you," but daddy I need you to take me to the store first. That way my Nanny can get her present, and she might stop all that crying. So can we go now, my daddy?

"Hello, my sweet uncles. Can I have . . . Oh, thank you all. I love you. See, daddy, come on all the ladies are all crying with my Nanny. By the time they stop crying we could have gone to the store and back to the house."

"Okay, but, my little one, why is your Nanny crying?"

"Oh, daddy, Mr. Larry, make my Nanny and all the ladies stop crying."

"Oh, I see. Well, let's go in the house and see what your mother and your Nanny are crying about. Also, let's if your mother needs something from the store and if Mark wants to go to the store, too. Okay?" Brian looks at Larry with a small smile on his face.

He and the little one walk into the house.

"Mark, would you like to go with me and your sister to the store?"

Brian went over to his other and wife.

I had better go into the house to see about Kara and if she's alright," said Mr. Blackwell.

All the men turned and looked at Larry and started to laugh at him. No one was moving. They all remain seated in their chair.

"Do have a seat, Larry. Do you see anyone else moving to see why the ladies are crying?" asked Brian.

"Look at you with a half smile, but, my boy, also know the rule. But you did talk to that sweet little angel, right?"

"Yes," said Larry.

"Well, young man, we all love that little angel. Now you think real good. Now who told you the ladies were crying in the house? Are you thinking, yes?"

"Oh, right. If my sweet, little angel, the messenger, hadn't come out the house looking for her daddy, we would not know anything about the ladies. But, she was looking for her daddy, and she saw you. Understand me, okay?

"So, my little one was already mad with you because she thinks you made her Nanny and all the ladies cry. She overheard the ladies talking, and your name was called. So my little angel came to tell you off about her Nanny."

"Larry, I need you to listen to me real good now. There are eight women inside that house now. If you like your life and would also like to see tomorrow, you will keep yourself right out here with the rest of the man. And mind your own business. Never go check on your lady when she is with her folks because, man, one will start to cry, and all will cry. One will start laughing, and all do the same. One giggling and they all start to giggling. So, you stay the hell away. That is for sure, or you are likely to get your feelings hurt real bad. So, Mr. Larry, if you do like we do, you will stay out the kitchen until your ladies call you. That way you will live much longer. So, if I was you, I would make myself look busy like the other half of us. Man, just sit and talk about anything to take your mind off Kara," said Mr. Blackwell.

"Look, Larry, no hard feelings. Believe me, if you're sure you can hang around long enough, you will find out all about the lady. But, we can't tell you too much until we know you are a part of us. So, in the mean time make the best of it. Make yourself at home, and enjoy it while you can because the next time you see the lady it will be honey time. Honey, do this. Honey, can you? Honey, do that. Oh, honey! Larry, will you try to think back a little earlier in the morning when all the man were eating?

"In the dinner room," said Larry.

"Now, Larry, were there any ladies at the table with us? No! Good, now have you got the picture, my man? No women. So that means we the big bosses in the house. No man can tell the men a thing."

Everyone started laughing and looking at Larry.

"Look, you just take it as it comes along. The woman run the show around here and at all the houses."

"Look, my young lady is inside the house with all of them talking and crying. I don't need that. Oh, her comes my mother," said John.

"Oh Larry, will you come into the house for a few minutes," said Kara.

"Oh, hell, man, your ass is ice."

Everyone was laughing at Larry.

"Well, my man, you finally get a chance to go and see about your woman at last.

"Well, Willie, it's honey time. We need to go and get that meat before the door closes again on us," said John.

"Also, Larry, you could stop all that worrying about your baby."

"Oh, boy," said Ronald.

"Hello, Larry, how are you today? I see you are hanging out with the boys," said Kara.

"Oh yeah, right. I am hanging out with the men, and you didn't ever tell me this morning that you were cooking breakfast. It was some good, too. Also, baby, why were you crying a few minutes ago in the kitchen, you and the other ladies, Kara?"

"Oh, no. My little angel was outside already talking her little head off. Look, Larry, I always cry when I am happy about something. There was no problem with me at the time, Larry. I am just a cry baby. I cry all the time," said Kara.

"Look at me, Kara. Do I look like somebody's big ass fool to you? Now, Kara, remember you are talking to me, Larry Grant. Your little angel, as you call her, came running outside and saw me. She was nice and walked over to me to tell me you were crying and that all the ladies were also crying. Can you guess, Kara, who the big bad man was? Kara, the mean, old man made her Nanny cry, and she did not like to see her Nanny cry at all. You know something, Kara? I can help you or hold you. So please talk to me. I hurt when you hurt, baby. So do talk to me now," said Larry.

"Look, we will have to talk tonight. Okay? My mother needs to have a little talk with you right now. So do come with me. She is waiting for you in the living room. I need to help my father get the food together. I will see you outside, okay," asked Kara.

She walked outside to the patio and left Larry standing in the room.

"Come over here, Larry, and have a seat. We need to talk. I do not know much about you at all. I can only go by what my children tell me about you. So, I am hoping this here talk with you will help me out some. Now, I did have a talk with Willie and Helen about you. Now Willie, he speaks very highly of you. So I will be taking his word at face value. I took my child's word until I could talk to you face to face to get your answer. I also know that my husband has already had his talk with you. So, Larry, it is time me and you talk man to woman."

"I will put my few words into the same pot, also. Now it is okay if I call you Larry?"

"Oh, yes, madam."

"Good, now you can call me mom. That's what all the other children call me. Good now that's out the way. Now, Larry, I am going by what you are telling me today. I am taking your word now. No one else. So, Larry, I am trusting you with my baby. I do hope my confidence in you does not turn out to be on the fear side. I know I am telling you right now that I will not see my baby hurt again by no one. If so, I will be hurting back myself. So I am asking you as a very concerned mother and a worried one. Now, my baby seems to be very happy now days. So you must be doing something right. I am hoping that you will keep on making sure she stays that way. Now her father and I kind of cut our month vacation kind of short this time to come back home so that our grandchild, Mr. Brian, would not cause any kind of trouble for his mother this time. So we up and took the next plane back home."

"Kara called and said you were coming over for a Sunday dinner, but she did sound too good. Her father did like the sound of her voice. No one knew that we were coming home but my son, Timothy. You met him that Sunday. He was at the airport to pick us up. No one would had known we walked in the house. After everybody had got there, that husband of my just had to have that old-fashioned breakfast that morning. So I had to call Kara to tell her we were home, and she will have to cook her father his fat breakfast that morning. So now she knows that here parents are back in town. Now that all the others know we are back, you can tell the hold tribe knows. So, the house is full with the family. Everybody has been looking right in your face.

CHAPTER TEN

"Well, Larry, you already saw that. I bet you were just looking for her children. But you had the whole family, right?"

"Yes, madam, you know, come to come to think about it. Not one person asked why we were home so early. We were on that long monthly vacation. We lost some money by cutting it so short, but my child comes first. Everyone was acting so happy to see us back at home. So not a soul said a word. You know, Larry, you have to see things in Brian's eyes. He and his father are very close. No space between the two. No one can come between them two. Now that Mike has been talking to my Brian, he is making him think his mother and he are going back together one day, but we all know that is never going to happen, like a cold day in hell. He has hurt my baby one time too many times, and Brian knows all this."

"There's no if, and, or but about it. No turning back to no old past. Kara just up one day and closed herself away from the world. All she would do was go to work, come back home, and lock herself away. She refused to go out or date. Pam and Ronald asked her to take a two week vacation with them, and she said no thank you. The same with the rest of the family. It was always a no thank you. She would never say yes. Now, for the first time, you came along. Helen feels bad that she said no but she said no in a kind of way that she had never talked to Helen before. She said some sharp word to her in a bitter way. The three girls have been best friends for days. Once Helen was walking around crying and made Willie unhappy."

"So, Mr. Willie just refused to hear anymore. So he just walked in on her at work one day and told Kara she needed to stop and listen to him. He had a nice, long talk with her, and she finally said yes. Now it was overnight, but she didn't think very carefully about it before she said yes to Willie. She thought about what Willie said to her for a while. Larry, you have come along and opened that long-closed door and put some light in her life once again. So please don't let that same door suddenly close. You will have to try and keep it open at all times. I need you to try not to make anymore dark days for her. If you can help it, she needs lots of good days and happy ones too, Larry."

"Now, I think you really care for my baby girl. If you didn't I know for a fact you wouldn't be taking her on a two week vacation. You know something. I can trust you with my daughter, and I hope my confidence in you does not turn out to be a big mess. No my fear on the outcome. Matter of fact, I will not be able to see my baby hurt again. This time I will hurt back, and I mean really hurt, too, Larry. Now my Brian and Diane kind of take a long time to get to like a person, but the two will soon come around. Brian has started to like you a little bit."

"Larry, there is one thing I need to know about you. Now only you can be the one to answer this question. I need you to be for real now. No lies. Larry, do you really care for my Kara for herself or are you just acting like you care because you a good friend to Helen and Willie? You do not need to feel sorry for my child, or just out to help out an old buddy. Because it you are young man, you just walk the hell out that door right now and never ever look back because, young man, I have a few guns laying around in the house. I will put a few holes in your ass over my child now, any of my children. You know something, Larry? I went to get a hold of that Mike. I was heading to that man, but Helen had to be home that day, and she saw me put the gun in the car. And she called Willie. She should have been at work that day."

He got to him before I did because I was going to put a few shoots in Mr. Mike. I was not going to miss him. Matter of fact, I was out for his blood that day. I was out to endanger his body like he did to my child, but Willie stopped me. Mike will not cross my path. We do not come into any contact or pass each other every day. I am still out to get him. Look, I am an old lady. I will go crazy as hell and kill you over my children. So, I hope you are listening to me very close, Mr. Larry Grant. You make very sure that you are playing with a full deck and not a half one. If you are, all hell will suddenly break lose on your ass, my boy."

"So I am askng you as nice as I can, Larry. I am not cutting no corners or around no corners to get to the safely point. I take it as it comes, big or small. We all cried today, and laughed together. Now we are so happy for Kara. Now that crying today was happy. We do not need no sad crying, okay, Larry," said Mrs. Blackwell.

"Oh, Mrs. Blackwell, I was worried about Kara. When the Little one came out and said I was the one who made her Nanny cry, I needed to know what had I did. You asked me a few question about my life."

"Well, one of your questions I can answer right now, Mrs. Blackwell. I really care for your daughter, Kara. She is the only woman in my life but my mother. You know, Mrs. Blackwell, I am very glad that I met her through Willie and Helen. That way I know I found myself a good woman now. Willie talked about Kara all the time. I knew all about Kara way before I saw her. I had seen so many pictures of the three ladies. So one day, I asked Helen to bring her over so I could meet her and her family. But she didn't bring the family over to meet me. I have known her for a long time," said Larry. "Now your number two question is I am not an actor. I can't act at all. Now do not get me wrong. I do like women, but at this time I have found my dream girl for keeps. And I will never hurt her. I do love your daughter, and that is between you and me in confidence like a secret. So if anyone gets hurt, it would be me, not your Kara. Also between you and me, only you know how I feel for Kara. I talk to Willie all the time, but I never told him my feelings. Kara does not no how much I care for her. She is still afraid to trust any man right now, but I am hoping by the time we get back home she will have some kind of feelings for me, too. Like showing some kind of love toward me, and she will start to believe in me and not be afraid or me. I really care for that woman," said Larry.

"Well, well, Mr. Larry, I really believe that you do care for my daughter the way you are talking. Now that really makes me feel a whole lot better about you, and that makes me a very happy mother. I really thank you for this here talk. I couldn't ask for anymore than that from you. Mr. Larry, you said you are man of your word. So now we are all finished with our little talk. So I am going to welcome you to my little family with open arms. I know my husband has already talked to you and welcomed you already into the family. Now that there is no way you are turning around, my young man. You are a part of this here Blackwell family. Now you go and find your woman, and I will get me some rest before it's time to eat."

"I need a short nap. I also heard you asking Kara about her crying. I think you already worry about her. So you need to go and get your woman and talk to her alone. Larry, will you tell my children I need a short time out?" said Mrs. Blackwell.

She went to her room and Larry walked out the door to look for Kara. He saw her sitting on the patio with Helen, Pam, and her little angel sitting on her lap kissing her all over her face. He was smiling just to see her look so beautiful and hope she was all his. He would just love to pick her up and walk away right now before tomorrow. But he knew that her family wouldn't like that too much.

"Oh well, I can wait one day," he smiled to himself. "I will have you all to myself tomorrow. No family to come along."

He walked over to Kara.

"Well, hello ladies, nice to see all of you beautiful ladies today. And how is my beautiful little one this time?" asked Larry.

"Oh, my Nanny, he called me his little one and also said beautiful, too. He is nice now my Nanny," said Michele.

"Yes," said all the ladies, "And hello to you, too, Mr. Larry. I see she is all finished talking to you. So you can come and sit with the ladies for a few minutes. My little angel has something to tell you. Right, my little one?" said Kara.

"Yes, my Nanny." Mr. Larry, my Nanny said that I have to apologize to you about me telling you that you made my Nanny and my other moms cry. I am very sorry that I said something like that to you, Mr. Larry. Oh, but where is my other Nanny. Did you make her cry, too? I do not see my Nanny," said Michele.

"Oh, no, little one, your other Nanny is taking a nap. She needed to rest some. Is that okay with you, Miss Thang? You are giving me a hard time today," said Larry.

"Okay, Michele, you go and find your brother and play with him," said Kara.

"Oh right, my Nanny and all my moms. Love you all."

"Larry that little angel is getting to you. She looks like she will be your number one girl."

Everybody just laughed at Larry.

"So, Mr. Larry, didn't our mother welcome you to the family, or are you still on the wait list? Try to make it in somehow," said Helen.

"Oh, yes, she did, but, Helen, your mother can be a hard case to crack. Now she can lay down some very, heavy law when it comes down to her daughter. Now that little lady, she does not take any mess from anyone. She told me she will hurt me if I hurt her child or anyone in her family.

"Helen, I like her. She's my kind of person. She doesn't take any prisoners," said Larry.

"Yes, you are right about her. Mom does speak her mind about all of her family. But I see you are welcome to the family, and now you talk about taking our mom on, too. My God, man, anyone of the Blackwell's are enough for you. My, you get Kara. Now you lure our mom along, okay," said Pam. Laughing, "Well, Mr. Larry, you are all set to take our Kara away for two long-ass weeks, and you didn't even ask anyone of us to go with you on this here trip with you and Kara. You just up and make all kinds of plans without talk to her family about this here trip. Do you know that Kara has never been away from home before alone? So, you make sure you take damn good care of our Kara, or we will well have to talk to the head boss, okay, Mr. Larry? We ladies can't see her at all tomorrow. The men said we ladies cried too much, so daddy told us to say our good bye and love you's today."

"And I do not like to say no, but I am hoping to see you on down that road. So, we ladies will say our bon voyage tonight to you two. You know something, Larry. You are much happier today than you were the other day. Our mom must have told you something very good because today you are a very happy man," said Pam.

"Yes, Larry, you are a lot happier today. Oh, Kara, did you throw this poor man all your love this way? Girl, you know the price you have to pay, and you've never been rocked enough to play big girl games with Mr. Larry," said Carol.

All the ladies came over to sit down and started talking with Larry and Kara. Everybody was laughing.

"Oh right, now children, you leave the two alone. Now my Kara is going to win. Let her have a natural ball, and Pam, you just stop that talk about you want to go on this trip. You are not going, so stop talking about it now. Samuel, is that meat well enough to eat? I am so hungry! I am starving from your good food cooking on the grill."

"Come on, Mrs. Pam, Mrs. Helen, and also Ms. Carol. Get the food together so we can eat. Larry, I told you to get your woman and go talk. I mean to leave the house. So you and Kara you don't exist any more. Now clean up your little trouble. Some food will be here. Come on, ladies. Mom needs you. Right now. You and the other ladies get the table set up and everything together. Oh, yes, you men, it that time. You have been taking it to easy today, so let's move it. All the dark clouds have rolled away for this here family. So, now, let's have an enjoying day. No more crying. They will sail away with lots of hugging and kissing tonight."

"Brian, you go inside the house and get that champagne and put it on ice and let it get cold. You all listen to me. I am taking a chance today on Mr. Larry Grant. He said something by accident that happened to change things a little. You know I took a nap, and now I am see things a hold lot different but in a new, fresh way. Now I need everybody to stop and listen to me. Like I said before, the dark clouds have rolled away for us. I am seeing things in a better light than before. I do see everything a whole lots different than before. Now we all will start today seeing people in a better way like this new one, not the old one. We had enough hurt in this here family."

"We are a very close family. We can't close ourselves off for the rest of the world with Kara. So it is time to open that door to some light. Samuel, you and I are open to Larry. He is a good man. He talked to me just like my Willie and Ronald. He didn't hold back. I like that about him, Samuel. The man knows what he wants out of life, and that one thing he wants is your daughter. Now let's get this here food all together before Kara and Larry get back to the house," said Mrs. Blackwell.

"Mom, we need to get some wine for Larry. He likes wine and not champagne. So one of us needs to go to the store," said Carol.

"Mom, are we celebrating something tonight that we need some wine and champagne?" asked Diana.

"Yes, my child, we are going to celebrate that your mother is finally flying out of the nest. So, we need to help make her very happy. This time we might have a happy ending."

Kara, you need to talk to me, baby. Why were you crying? Some your little angel said you called my name. She was mad with me so do tell me all about it. Are you afraid to go along with me on this here cruise by yourself? Look here, my love, I would never hurt you or leave your side. I will be with you at all times, Kara. I had already told you before, if you hurt, I hurt, too. Look at me, Kara. You are my woman, and I will be glad to tell the world that you are all mine, no half stepping at all, baby. So, you can stop all your tears. I am your man. You have nothing to worry about. We are together and cannot be divided without hurting both of us. No more cloudy days for you, my love.

"Kara, I'm telling you right now that I am a damn, jealous man over my woman. I do not play around. I pay to be the boss at all times. One day you will see for yourself what I am talking about, and you will understand if there's anything you need to know about me, you just ask me. I will be very glad to answer any question you need to know about me. I do not have a thing to hide from you. Look, I asked John to take over your business. I also put a laptop computer in my bag. So if you need to solve some of your affairs you can process them on the ship. See, I am looking out for you, baby. I want you to enjoy this here cruise. You need to start feeling good about yourself, baby. You need to live again."

"You have been so busy taking care of your business that you have not taken any time off for your own self. So, I come along now, and we are on our way on a cruise. Kara, you know something? You have been my dream girl for a few years, but you did not want to be my dream girl. You didn't even want to meet me at all, but, thank the Lord, Willie didn't give up on you. Kara, I will give my life for you, baby. I am looking for you to open that door, one day, to your heart. I need you to be loving for me. I am the man for you, Kara. Now I ain't too proud to beg, but, baby, father down that road you need to remember there is no turning back."

You might get lonesome down that long road all by yourself. You just might need someone to come along to help you down that long, dark road. I am that somebody, baby. We can make it together, my love. I have been needing you for a very long time. Now together we can make it to the end of the road and never look back at the life before, my baby girl. Oh, love, we need to get back to the house before your mother sends Brian after us, and that would not be too good," said Larry.

"You are right about going home, but you know something, Larry? You have done all the talking today, but, now, according to you, we seem to been playing some careful game. Well, Mr. Larry, we do have two week together on a ship, right? Well, I will be finding out before we return back home. Actions do speak much louder than words."

"So you make sure you show me some of this except now you need to start on day one. I'm no pushover anymore, Larry. You are right about this long road. We all have been somebody's fool, but no more. Yes, we all play some kind of foolish game but no more. Today I am starting to push back. If you push my button I am going to push right back."

Suddenly, she was getting sharp pains in her chest. She was feeling that nervous feeling again. Every nerve was acting up. She was getting that emotional feeling. Oh my, he had a lot of nerve going where he wasn't wanted. Now it was the time to show her strength with this man. She knew that her whole body always turning to water. If he only knew what he did to her. He would be just laughing at her. He need only say a few words to her, and she was no good. She was thinking to herself that she did hear Larry call her name.

She was way out in left field. She didn't even see the ball fly right by her eye. Larry called her again. This time she looked at him, said "Yes, Larry."

"Baby, what's the matter with you? Are you getting sick or something? You look a little on the hot side. You started changing color on me. You lost your color and became mighty pale, baby. Now you tell me what is the matter with you. Are you mad with me about something I said to you? Now let me have it, alright? Now if you are mad with me, tell me now. Don't hold anything back, okay? I need to know what you are thinking about. Right now, I have already told you all about my life. I will never lie to you about anything. I care too much about you to ever tell you a lie. So, Kara, please talk to me baby. Come on, my love, let me take you back home. But you can't look like that or your family will think I hurt you."

He put his arms around her. He was holding Kara in his arms. "My God, I love this here woman, but what can I do when she won't tell me anything. But something is wrong with her. She didn't turn so pale for nothing. She just looked at me like I had two heads on my shoulders. Hell, she's right about one thing. We do have two weeks to get to know each other, but, if not, I will take another week to make sure she is my woman and then no turning back."

"That man must have treated her mighty bad. I would like to get my hands on that man for hurting my baby. She does not trust me too much, but before this trip is over with, she will. Kara, baby, we are at the house. Come on, my love, give me a big kiss, and put that big smile on your face so your family will not think I did something to you. At last your color had come back in your face."

"Well, hello, you two love birds. I see you two are already back now. Just know you two are on the same page in your life by now with that big, old smile on your two faces," said Mrs. Blackwell.

Larry still had his arm around Kara's waist. He would not let her go, he said to himself. He just wished that he was on that same page she was on. But he was still on the outside trying to look in.

"Come on, everybody, it is about time to start having a good time this evening. Now, my baby never took a nice vacation before like this one. So it is time that we all gave her this special occasion. So now we all are going too celebrate this vacation with her and Larry."

"Samuel, our baby is about to fly away from us and her happy, little nest that has sheltered her for so long. We all have a helping hand, and it is long over due. So, everyone, come and get a glass of wine or champagne, and we will all toast to the couple," said Mrs. Blackwell.

"Well, my mother, I am so happy for you and Larry on this here cruise. I know Pop-pop and Nanny have already talked and welcomed you to the family, but, Larry, I am her oldest son. So I think I also need to pay my respects by welcoming you to the Baker family. Also, there are no hard feelings between you and I. We just started off on the wrong foot. Just make sure that woman is happy. That's all we ask of you," said Brain.

He kissed his mother and shook hands with Larry.

"Brian, I really appreciate that you welcome me to the Baker family. That really makes me feel real good about you and me as men. Thank you very much, man," said Larry.

"Kara, are you alright now, baby? Look, I need to know how you feel. All your family is looking right at me," said Larry.

"Yes, I am. Did you tell me to put a big-ass smile on my face? Well, it is still there."

He started laughing and both of them was laughing.

"Okay, Larry. I am just fine. So you go and talk to the men, and I will go and talk to the ladies," said Kara.

"Okay, just keep that pretty smile on that beautiful face of yours. Well, ladies, I am going to give you my woman for a few hours, and I will be back to get my baby," said Larry.

All the women started to laugh.

"Well, we all thank you so much, Mr. Larry, for letting us have your woman for a few hours. Now that is so nice of you to do that for us little old ladies," said Pam. "Now that was so sweet!"

"You all are so welcome," said Larry and was heading towards the pond where the men were.

The small one was in the sandbox playing, and Mrs. Blackwell was seated watching the small one. Larry walked over to the pond where he sat down and started talking to the men. All the ladies gathered around Kara. Everyone started talking and laughing.

"So, my mother, are you already for this trip? Is all of your packing finished, and you're sure you have everything. You're not leaving anything? Did you recheck to make sure you have it all? And guess what we all did for you? I went to mom's shop and got you one of the hottest and sexiest night gowns for you. We all got it for you, and some warm, sex lotion to put on your and his body. That's when the fun starts. Mother, you will be a knockout," said Carol.

"Yes, baby girl, you will be one sexy-ass woman. You will have to look sexy as hell. You will knock his lights out. He already knocks himself out over you as it is. You just stand with that big-ass smile on your face. You know something. Helen, can't you remember when we all were in college together. We always sent you to get some food and everything we would need. We were always nice and sent you to get it. She would put that big-ass smile on her face."

That smile would always get to the men. Now Kara, you just had that smile on your face a few minutes ago. So would you like to tell me what the hell have you done this time? I do hope you did tell Larry about your smile," said Pam.

"Oh, hell no, I was smiling so that the old boy would stop talking so much. The man never shuts up. I just couldn't take it anymore. Poor me couldn't get one word in. He just keeps on talking. I will need something to slow that mouth of his up. So, a sexy night gown will stop him from talking so much. We might have a good vacation. After all, I need you ladies to listen to this now. Mr. Larry still makes every cell in my body turn to liquid. I still can talk to the man. He just makes me mad as hell and so nervous that my body still can't take this man. So what am I going to do about that? You ladies need to help poor me. I only have eight more hours to go, and I will be Mr. Grant's woman. Just me and the king all alone on a big-ass ship. We will be sailing away from everyone. My God, I am sailing at noon tomorrow. The closer the time comes, the more nervous I get.

"Larry told me no more weeping and crying this evening. Hell, the poor man is asking for the wrong thing. If we started to laugh that leads to giggling and that leads to crying," said Kara.

"You poor, little girl. Your man has got a big ass problem on his hands. He will find out that you cried by just looking at you. Hell, he's got a long road to cross before he gets you to stop crying. We all tried to stop you from crying, but it didn't work. So, who does he think he is? The control king?" said Diana.

All the ladies started laughing.

"Okay, let's all have one good, old, strong drink. That way, we will complete this trip. So come on, everyone, let's go into the house to the bar and fix us some mix drinks and have a bit of fun before it's time for Mr. Grant to come and get his woman. So let's go and let our hair down. No one has to drive a vehicle home. We already are at home. We can all sleep right here on the floor as we have done so many times."

"Mother just closed the door and always said, Night girls" but daddy would come and check out everything to make sure we didn't have any boys in the room with us. He would always lock the windows and walk out with a smile on his face. You know something? We did have some boys outside, but we could not open the door or the window. We just talked through the window. Now those were some good old days," said Helen.

"Mrs. Helen, how did you three become sisters? You three are so close," said Lillian.

"Kara lived in the same community. Her father was the dentist in the center."

"One day, Pam and I went to the dentist to get our teeth checked, and we saw Kara. She was working for her father. Pam and I were already best friends. We started talking to Kara. We liked her right away, so we three became the best of friends. We also started to work in the dentist office, too. Kara's mother and father took us in, and we became her sisters. So that's how they became our parents. They are the best. No problem is too big for the Blackwells. Lillian, you will love this family. Everyone loves one another. A big happy family all the time. Like we said, one cries and all cry, one hurts and all hurt. That's how close this family is. Mary loves us, alright?"

"Yes, I do. I never cried so much until I married into this family, but I love everyone."

"Mother, and Mom Blackwell are the only mothers I have. They are my life. You will love this family. You and Larry are newcomers, but you will be alright," said Mary.

"Yes, Lillian, if John and Carol like you, my girl, you are home free. That mean the rest will like you," said Helen.

"Yes, I love all you guys. I will stay at Larry's house tonight. You know, his home is much closer to the airport than my house is, and we need to be at the airport by 5 am. I am too afraid to sleep tonight, so Diana, baby, do fix your mother a good, strong drink. I need it to help my nerves. Nevertheless, you and Carol do have a good time in France. Diana, baby, I love you. I want you to have a good time in life, too, my love. I know you talked to daddy about this trip. I know you also said that you never want to go back to France. But baby, that was a long time ago. Look love, your old mother is making a move and so are you. We will walk down this road together, my love."

"Okay, your mother just loves her children, and I would like for them to have the best at all times. That's all, love," said Kara. "Oh, mother, I love you, too, and I do thank you for this trip to France. Who knows? I might just find myself a good-looking, rich, white boy and bring him home and make my daddy and Brian mad as hell. The two old fools always said I didn't like black men. I only date very good-looking light-skinned men," said Diana.

"Oh hell, Diana, a man is a man. The all put it in the same way. Some are small, and some are big as hell, but a man is a man, and a woman is a woman. The hell with the damn color. We are all the same in God's eyes," said Carol.

"Carol, baby, why are you getting mad? I have always taught you kids better than that. We never talk about color. Your daddy has his own problems all by himself. Now Brian, he is a difficult person. Brian is the kind that likes to pick out your man for you."

"If he could, that would really make him very happy, and every thing would fall right into his hands. Now Mary, she loves her man, so she puts up with her man. Poor thing is her problem, but we all love him, too. So come on now, you two, it was only a little mistake on Carol's part. She had no right to say that to you. For now on, no one has a reason to drop that on anyone again. I have kept this away from everybody until today. I met this nice man one day. He came into my office to book a seven day cruise to one of the islands. Two weeks later he walked back into the office. We started talking and became very good friends. You know, I had just started my business. It wasn't doing too good or bad at the time, but I just held my head up out the water. I could pay some of my bills and take care of my children. Mike hadn't been too long left me for some hot momma. Now he takes care of his house and children, but not me."

"He didn't want me to have a job. I needed to come to him for money. I needed, but that was a no no. So my friend started calling and coming by to see me. He would ask me how my business was coming along. He could see I wasn't doing too good. So, one day, he just came out and told me he was bringing in me some good business. He liked me, and I needed his help. Girl, I said yes, I did need his help. Month before last I was up to my eyeballs with business. I was booking cruises to foreign countries left and right. I was booking all over the world. I needed some help. So I put John and the girls to work. Brian was away in college. The three had one more year to go in high school. So I could use them for a little while until I could get my dear friend to help me get my business up off the ground."

"Now we were becoming very close friends. We started going out together to some nice, French restaurants sometimes or just out for a few drinks. I enjoyed being out with him. We laughed and talked, and he listened to me talk about some of everything. He has the most beautiful smile. I love being around him. He came by early one morning. He was going out of town to a meeting, something to do with his business. He asked could I go with him. The man was looking in my eyes. The next thing I knew, I was in his arms. He was kissing me, and I was kissing back. I never felt so good! I wanted him to kiss me. I do not know where that damn Mike came from, but the man started saying, "Hey, you! She is not available. She is still my wife. You have a second to take your damn hands off that woman." He was trying to get tough and violent by calling the man a name."

"Now Mike is a grown man, but that day he was still growing up. He said he has seen me with that man a couple of times. So he thought it was time to stop me from seeing him before I made a big fool out of myself. My friend cut down on some of his visits. He still calls and asks me do I need anything. I really liked that man. I miss him so bad. He moved to another state. He e-mails once a week, but it's not like seeing the man," said Kara.

"Oh, my God, you poor girl. You could tell your two best friends about this man, Kara. Was this man a B bro or an A bro?"

asked Pam.

"Oh, yes, he was an A bro, but a sweet bro. Never said anything about sex. He never asked me to go to bed with me. That was the first time he had ever kissed me. We had talked for four months. At the most, we were good friends.

I couldn't tell you two anything about my friend. I had to keep it to myself because, number one, he was a young, white man, and he was only five years older than my Brian. You two would really have thought I was crazy as hell. So I kept my secret to myself. Carefully hid away from you two whether you two were my best friends or not. You might have had a little more to say, and I did need to hear your side. So, I kept it hid away until now."

"But that Mike was so mad with me that day. He was talking about I was cheating on him. My God, the man had been cheating on me from day one. We were having some strong words with each other. I told him to get the hell out of my office and never come back. The man just looked at me and said, "Now Kara, I am still your husband until the end of time. I will never give you a divorce. You know me. I started to cry like a big fool. Mike took me in his strong arms. I always love those arms of his, so big and strong. It had been so long since Mike had held me like that. I liked it and cried like some fool-ass woman."

"He said," Baby, you know I am so sorry the way I was acting, but that damn, white man with his arms and lips on you. The man was kissing you, and you were kissing the man back. Damn, Kara, you never kiss me like that. So I saw red right there, woman. I could have killed you and him. We are only separated, not divorced. Kara, you are still my wife. I love you, baby. Please take me back. Hell, I stopped crying then, pushed him back, and looked right in his face and said, "You listen to me real good, Mr. Mike Baker. I have already taken you back twice, and both times you turned right around and did the same thing all over again. So, Mr. Baker, hell no. Not again." So I nicely walked to the door to open it and said to Mr. Baker, "Now you be nice and walk out this here door. Please do not come back anymore.""

"Mike, I had six years of your treatment. I do not need one more day of your sweet, little lies, but that still didn't stop the man from coming by. He thought that my friend would be around, but he didn't come when Mike was around. But one day, my two, big, strong brothers stopped by, and Mr. Mike started running that big mouth of his, and he said the wrong thing to Willie and Ronald. That day he started saying that that so-called brother of mine would mind their own business, that he would be with his wife today. "You two need to keep your nose out of my personal business. She is my wife, not yours. So keep the hell out of my damn personal life," he was saying. Ronald told me to go into my office and close the door. Ronald told Willie to go out and Mike because he going to hit Mike."

The three men went outside. Ronald closed the door behind the three. Mike was getting so tough and violent. I did not know that Mike hated you four, and he is trying to start the children to also hate you four. But it didn't work out too good for Mr. Mike. I know he stopped come by the office," said Kara.

"Oh, my sweet sister dear, let me tell you why Mr. Mike stopped by your office. This is a read good story, too. Now my man, Willie, was going to do some old knockout surgery on Mr. Mike. An operation that no man ever had before. Mr. Willie was going to give that man a sex change operation. The man would never be able to use it again at all on no woman. He would be just standing there looking like a big-ass fool," said Helen.

Everybody was so into Helen's story that no one heard Mrs. Blackwell come into the house.

CHAPTER ELEVEN

She walked into the room and just stood and listened to the conversation. Helen was just talking, everyone was laughing so hard at Helen, and no one saw her until she spoke to Helen.

"So, Mrs. Helen, you are a bad girl now. Not that I want Mike myself, but now you tell me your husband was going to do some good, old operation on that damn fool, Mike, but you wouldn't let me shoot the old dog. Everyone turned at the same time and looked at Mrs. Blackwell.

"Oh, my mother. When did you come into the house? And, mother, you wanted to kill my ex, too."

"Oh, my God, you people are all crazy as hell. If daddy hears you two talking like that he wouldn't like it to good. He does not like violence at all. We all will be in a world of trouble. That is for sure. I wouldn't have known about Willie until that day he was talking about getting my life together. So why did your husband treat my ex so bad?" asked Kara.

"Yes, baby, it took you a long time to open your eye to life. So do not close your eye anymore. Okay, my child? I came to get you all. It's that time to say all of our so longs and have a good time and kiss and hug and cry. Kara, so you are going to be staying at Larry's house tonight because he lives much closer to airport than you do. So that was a good idea since you two have to be at the airport at 5:00 a.m. tomorrow morning. Too early for me and your daddy. So we are ready to say our bon voyage to you and Larry. He is ready to go. You have to go by your house to get your bag. Kara, everything is alright, baby?"

"Oh, mom, we all make sure her bags were packed and ready to go," said Helen.

Well, that's good. So, come, everyone, let's go outside before Mr. Larry comes and gets his woman here. But, baby, put our jokes away. I've got some serious matters now, baby. Your mother wants you to go and have a real good time. Now no holding back at all, baby. You just go and enjoy life for a change. Now, we all love you, and you listen to me this one time. You have found yourself a good man, no half-ass one this time like before. This one really cares for you and only you, not the whole world. So, Kara, you just take it day by day, and try to enjoy every sweet minute of it, baby," said Mrs. Blackwell.

All the ladies went outside to say their bon voyage and say farewell. Little tears were shed. Everyone was saying goodbye and kissing and hugging and shaking hands with Kara and Larry. Brian walked over to his mother and was hugging and kissing her.

He said, "Mother, I am only a phone call away if you need me and, by the way, just how long are you going to be gone away from your family? You know you are a long way from home," said Brian.

Now here comes the two little ones and crying saying "My Nanny, take us with you. We will be so nice. We promise you." You won't even know we are with you, my Nanny. We love you, my Nanny."

"Come on, you two, before your Nanny starts to cry and me, too. I love you, mother and Larry. I know you will take good care of my mother. Larry, I know you said your woman but she was mine before yours, so you just remember that," said Brian.

"Okay, Mr. Lawman. You and your children go on back to the house. I love you, too, mother and have a good time. I will take care of everything on this end for you. So do not think about a thing on this end. Your son is on the job. You take care, too, Larry."

Everybody tells Kara to have a good time, but no one told you to have a good time. Just you better take care of my mother. We all just love her. That's all that matters, so just take care and have fun."

John kissed and hugged his mother and said, "Mother, we all love you," and he shook Larry's hand and said, "Man, I am calling it a night."

He walks away with tears in his eyes, too. He did not want his mother to see him crying, so he just walked over to his woman-friend, and the two walked into the house. Mr. Blackwell walked over to Larry and Kara saying, "All right, you two, it is getting on the late side. You two need to get into that car now. If not, you will be here all night. Somebody will be coming to talk about something to keep you here all night."

He shook Larry's hand and hugged and kissed Kara. He had tears in his eyes, also. Kara started to shed a few tears. This time she saw tears in her father's eyes.

"Bye, my love. Do have a good time, and, young man, you,

too, have a good time."

Mr. Blackwell walked away, not looking back at Larry and Kara. The whole Blackwell family walked into the house and closed the door. Kara and Larry drove away. Larry was so touched by the way everyone was so close to Kara. He already knew that if he thought about hurting Kara, he was a dead man. The whole Blackwell family would just kill him a hundred times and hang him up by his feet about that woman. First the sons, next the three brothers, and here come Mrs. Pam and Miss Diana. Now Carol, she's totally different. She needs my help. She's being so nice until she get her schooling. Now Mary, she just sitting and looking with a half-ass smile on her face like Kara. But that mom and pop, now you are in for a lot of ass kicking. My ass will be tick-tick like an old clock. So, I will be playing it safe, pushing no wrong button. She will be my woman, and all along the way, no misunderstanding on my part. That is for sure."

Early Sunday morning about 4:30 a.m., Kara and Larry had just arrived at the airport. They were going to take the aircraft to Orlando, Florida. So far, everything seemed to be moving along just fine. It was getting to be that time to start boarding the plane that was leaving for Orlando. The two were in first class on the plane. They two took their seats and sat down. Larry took hold of her hand.

"Oh, my baby, your hands are so cold. Are you feeling a little chilled? Oh, come to me, and let me put my arm around you and try to make my baby comfortable and warm. Would like a drink to also help you warm up some? I will call the flight attendant to bring us a drink. I sure could use a drink myself. Would you like to have a bourbon now? That would kind of warm you up and lift up your sweet spirit some," said Larry.

"Yes, you're right. I could use a small drink of bourbon. I'm getting a little on the hungry side. I need the food, first. Yes, do call the attendant. And Larry, I am a little on the cold side, too. Now I have not flown in a very long time. So I am a little on the nervous side, too. Now a few years ago, we all got married on the same day. The three couples went on a honeymoon together. That was a big day. I was young and in love. So, I didn't have time to get nervous, I guess," said Kara. The flight attendant brought their drinks and some food to eat.

"Kara, baby, are you tell me Willie, Helen, Pam, and Ronald and your ex got married at the same time?

"Yes."

"And you six also honeymooned together?"

"Yes?"

"So where did you six go?"

"We all went to Hawaii."

"So how long was the sweet honeymoon?"

"A week."

"So all your people stayed in Hawaii, and you came back home?"

"Yes, but the other couples still honeymooned."

"Kara, my love, I would like to know something about your married life. Now you do not have to answer or reply to my questions if you do not feel up to it, but, my love, I would like to know. Didn't you and Mike, honest truth, love each other? Now it is good to think about these questions because each of us faces similar issues in our lives today. You were trying to challenge your best girlfriend and looking at the marvelous future. There was a special role the four would be playing, and you would be left out. So, you just talked Mr. Mike right into saying "I do" to you. But, love, you never really looked into finding out the whole truth about your Mike. Did you try to learn something about the man before you said I do? I think you really didn't get to know your Mike very well, Kara. Your friends got married so you said "I do," too. Baby you sound like someone that will follow the crowd to the end. You might love him but not enough to get married. You two were unmatched. Neither one of you should have married in the first place."

"The man just up and married you, never loved you like a wife should be treated. That man walked all over you. He never stopped seeing other women. Kara, I am very sorry for saying this, but you should have never married in the first place. Oh, do not get me wrong or misunderstand me, the man might have loved you in his own way, but he is a big womanizer. You were not enough for him. Truthfully, the man was very careless. He might claim to love you, but how could he when he was always running down the wrong road. Always far away, far down the same old road. I am so very sorry that you were hurt by that man. But, baby, always try to remember that you will never lose what you ain't never had in the first place."

"The sun is always shining now. I wonder why! So now, if you truthfully try to cope with a man that has always treated you on the bad side, you tell me what kind of man is that? Oh, I was told he was a damn good man to his children and kept his home in top shape at all times. Oh, yes, now a man will always make sure that his home it taken good care of so other men will not come along and mess up his happy little home."

"Now, my man, he sure understood that he was wrong and also by not keeping up with his part of being married to you, but, my sweet love, I promise you, I will never let you get hurt again by no one, and, my love, that is my promise to you. The purpose is now to always try to make you happy and give you so much good love. Now, myself, I will try to fulfill your life in order to be happy. Baby, you are worthy everyday of your life. You honestly, truthfully need the right, careful love. You are a hard hearted woman, not easy, but a person that is heartwarming," replied Larry.

"Oh, my God, Larry. You sure can talk, but you just said that my husband was a big-ass womanizer. How did you know that Mr. Mike, my so called ex, was an everyday womanizer? How did you know that? Mike was never a faithful man to me. He started on day one being unfaithful to me and now just how did you know about it? Now I would like you to just answer my questions.

"I know Willie. I know he did not tell you everything," said Larry.

"Right, so would you like to try explaining that to me now, Mr. Larry?" replied Kara.

Now sometimes questions are best left unanswered. There are plenty of questions that can and would play with your mind my, kiddo. I know you wonder about lots of things when none of them help you out one bit. Right, my little love one? You keep right on asking, but you still won't get your answers. Let us consider that you have lots of doubt about me, but you still are at the same door wondering why I still won't tell you the words that you would like to hear.

"Yes, Kara, you do deserve the right to get some good pleasure somewhere along this road, but now you my just be looking for lots of trouble. Also by asking too many unnecessary questions can also bring back some unhappy memories. And you right wonder why this man is so mean to me? Now we do not need that now do we, Kara?" asked Larry.

"I can't win in your book, but just remember one thing. I will never be your enemy. Neither would I ever hurt you, and I will never let anyone hurt you in my lifetime. That if I am around in your sweet life, my love, the sun is shining in your heart all the time now. Just try to remember you are my woman. I will never get tired of giving you my love. Sometime it is best to try and cope with your own so-called personal problems. Now, I know that I still have not answered your questions, have I, my love?" asked Larry.

He put Kara in his arms and held her. He started kissing her. It was a long kiss. He looked in her eyes and said, "My love, one day I will give you that pleasure and sit you down and answer all your questions that you asked me this day, but I can't satisfy your demand today, my kiddo."

"Now, my sweet little woman, do you know that you were so hurt by because your two best girlfriends in the world were so happy and so much in love? The couples had a most wonderful for marriage, and it seemed like it was a marriage made in heaven. No one could be that happy, but your best friends did marry the two most wonderful men. You think now. That is in your little world. Kara, you need to stop and look back along that same road. No marriage is made to last forever, my love. Just because your best friend is still happily married that does not mean that you can't have the same thing one day. Your next go around may just be the best thing that ever happened. This one could be your soul mate."

Kara, it seems to you that the couple's lives are all complete at this time, and you just followed down the wrong path. You looked for that so-called everlasting, sweet marriage, too, but it did work out that way for you. Look at it this way. You will be looking at the man with your eyes open this time. So the next time Mr. Right comes along, you will be ready. This Mr. Right will be the one lasting to death do us part. Oh, my God, Kara. We are in Florida. My, that was mighty quick," said Larry.

Everyone was getting off the plane heading in different directions, but most of the people were heading the same way that Kara and Larry were heading. There was some bus waiting to take the people to the ship. Kara and Larry were among the people getting on the bus.

"Oh, Larry. It looks like everybody is getting on the bus."

"Yes, my love. Let's go so we can get us a seat together."

Larry helps Kara up into the bus. She walks into the bus, finds two seats, and she sits down. She was still on the nervous side. Kara had not talked too much on the plane because Larry had not given her too much of a chance. The man talked all the way to Florida. Now all she could do was just sit and listen like a nice, little, old lady is supposed to do, I guess. The man just talked and talked all the time. Now I will never get lonely. I will not need a TV or radio with him around me. I never knew a person could talk that much. He never closes that mouth of his. Hell, all the man had to do was answer one little question. Oh no, he just keep right on talking his damn head off. He needed to try and close that mouth of his sometimes. Maybe I will be able to put in one word."

"Oh, no way. The man talked all the way to the Florida airport. Now you can't tell me that ain't some talking! Now I no I will never get a chance to get lonely away from my home and my family not the way Mr. Larry keeps right on running his big mouth. I think the man just loves to talk or likes to hear himself talk. Yes, we are all on this overcrowded bus, and it is so hot! The thermometer reads about 80 or 90 degrees. It is mighty hot. I started out on the cold side. Now I am so hot. It seems like it takes such a long time to get to the ship, but it won't be too long now. I can see the big white and blue ship.

Now, boy, that is one big ship, and look at all the people gathering around that big boat. We are all standing, waiting to get on the ship. Now we all have to get in a line before anyone can get on this ship. There a few lines, and we all are moving mighty slow. It seems to be taking a long time to get on the boat. We're moving at less than the usual speed. It's like a motion picture or a tape in which the action is made to appear much slower than it actually is. We're making a little bit of progress now. Just looks like everyone is talking a mile a minute. All I can see is so many people. Everywhere and everybody is looking so happy today. It just seems like everyone has a big smile on his or her face, but poor me is the only one feeling so sad and blue. Still, every cell is trying to run away from me right now.

I need to put on one of them big, happy smiles on my face and make myself look happy for the time being anyway. It is a long two weeks on this ship. I sure can't be screaming and crying too big for my grandbaby. She don't ever cry. It's just me, so get it together, Kara. Right now, no more crying and put your head up high with a big smile. Well, at least we are at the ship deck. We are all getting ready to go aboard the big ship with all the rest of the happy-looking people.

CHAPTER TWELVE

Two crew members are standing at the entry of the deck to take your ticket or your passport.

Well, Larry has everything with him, so he will take care of everything, so I will just walk slow a little ahead of him until he comes up to me. We will get on the ship together. Now there was some more crew members also waiting to tell you where you're your cabin is. Ours is on the upper deck. One of the crew members took our bags to our room, and we followed him to our room.

We walked into the room. Boy, this was one big room! I can't believe that a cabin room could be this large on a ship. It even has a sitting room, too. The bedroom had two beds in it.

"Oh, thank you so much, Larry."

"Look, my love, I know you are not quite ready for one bed. Not yet. You need some time to adjust to the idea before you start to share a bed with a man right now. So I made sure that they put two beds in the room with us. But now if you should change your mind, I wouldn't say one word but just hold you all night with a big smile on my face. By the way you are treating me, it will never happen, right baby?"

He was laughing at Kara.

"But, my little Kara, I would never go out to hurt you at all. I value your kindness and honesty to the highest, my love. So take that funny look off of your face, baby," said Larry.

"Oh Larry, it has been a very long time since I shared a bed with a man."

She was trying so hard to keep her nerves from acting up on her too much. She just might start crying. She sure didn't need to start crying, not way out here on this ship.

She smiled at Larry and said," Oh Larry, let's go back on the deck and do some looking around and just wave at the people that we is leaving behind," said Kara.

Larry and Kara left the cabin and walked back on the deck hand and hand. There were still a lot of people standing at the end of the deck looking and waving at the people.

The people were waving to everybody. She had a happy smile on her face this time. She was starting to get a good feeling.

"Kara?"

"Yes, Larry."

"Look, baby, let's walk over to the table and sit down. You need to make that phone call to your family. You know everyone is still at your mother's house just waiting for your phone call. So, my love, here is my phone. You make your call now to your family. And I will go and try to find us something to eat and drink. So, my sweet lady, call that unhappy, waiting family of yours before they start to think I have pushed you overboard."

Larry was laughing at Kara. She had a funny look on here face, but he was still laughing at her. Miss Thing didn't seem to think it was funny at all.

She said, "Yes, right Mr. Larry, have your funny. Mine will be coming along."

"Just keep on remembering, you are here to have a good time and live a little, my child. So please try. I need you to promise me you will have some fun, okay? We all love you and likewise the same to Larry. Okay, my love. Do have a good time. So long, my love."

Kara was thinking to herself. They say life is a big, old gamble. So she guesses she will start to live again. She was smiling to herself.

"Well, Mr. Larry, you told me no turning back. So, it's time I make the best of it," said Kara.

She was not too nervous right now. She was feeling so much better now since she talked to her family. Larry walked back to Kara with two drinks and some food on a tray with a smile on his face.

"Well, love, did you find everybody in a good mood? You gave all the good news and bad news to your family. I see you are not crying, so that must mean your worried family is much happier, too now since you called to tell them everything. I hope everyone is very happy now."

"So, my Kara, do I have you all to myself now, and no more of your family popping up out some hideaway corner? Or you and the ladies somewhere crying?"

He started laughing again.

"So, my love, I finally have you all to myself so far away from your family for two wonderful weeks. I do not have to share you at all. It is my time after all. Baby, you know I'm ready for you. I hope you are all ready for me to make love to you.

Larry looked at Kara and started laughing.

"We do need to spend some time together, just you and I. We need to know more about each other, and this the best time for me to get to know you so much better. No job! No phone calls! Just me and you out here on this big, wide ocean with all the fresh, salty air. Just a big, open sea, baby. I love the ocean. Baby, I try to make most of my travel by sea, when I can. You know Kara, I think you just might like it, too, by the time we get back home. The sea is so quiet and calm you can be at peace here in all the silence. You know, at night it is so much better. Especially when the fine mist sprays all on your face. It feels so good," said Larry.

He was quiet now looking out at the sea thinking with a smile on his face. He was not talking for once. Kara was also doing the same thing. She was also looking out at the sea. She was smiling. She had never seen so much water before. She was still, miles from land, no family, just lot of people and Larry. She just might like this trip after all. At last her nerves had quieted down some, and she felt so much better now. She touched Larry on the arm.

"Oh, Larry, let's go back to the room and change our clothes to something that is much cooler. My clothes are too hot for right now. So let's eat up and either way, let's go and get much more comfortable for a change," said Kara.

"Oh, now, that is good news to my ears, but, baby, first we need to go to the lounge to get something taken care of first. Like our acting before doing anything else, like our voucher, and check-in for our dinner area and yes, we definitely can go back to the cabin. I need a nap, you know. Now we can nap, or we can make some crazy love."

Larry was looking at the look on Kara's face.

"Just go and have a big toast with that champagne I saw in the room. We could make a nice, old toast to each other until it's time to go to dinner."

He was just laughing at Kara.

"Oh, come on, baby, you do need to loosen up some. It has been a long time since you had any fun, woman. You need to start right now."

"With me, you also need to try to laugh a little more. You are too uptight. You need to let yourself overflow. Let everything run out, or you let your wings spread out beyond. No more hiding away for this beautiful world, my love. You have been a lonesome woman for a long time, and your family is somewhere around to protect you from everything. So from now on you will be my woman to be protected for two wonderful weeks. Oh, boy. No Helen or Ms. Pam and special Mr. Brian somewhere around watching over my back. So Ms. Kara, I will be your bodyguard. Look here, Kara. What I'm trying to tell you is I want to be the one who takes care of you and keeps all the bad wolves away for your door."

"So, come, my love, let's take this nice walk down to the lounge, and let me take care of my business so we can go to bed," he laughs and walks away for Kara.

She walks, looks around, and she saw a man at the end of the hall. He was taking some people's picture, so she decided to have some pictures made to send back home to the family. She and Larry will take some together. Larry was finishing taking care of his business. He walked over to Kara and put his arm around her waist.

"Oh, Larry, let's take a picture, you and me, that we can send back home to the family," said Kara.

"Oh that is so nice of you, Kara, to want to send some pictures back home to your family of you, but why? You didn't say anything about a picture of me for all the family," said Larry.

Kara was laughing at Larry this time. Now it was on the other foot.

"Oh, Larry, you didn't say it right. I'm here with you, love, so why do you need a picture? If you do, I will try to put you on the list with the rest of the family."

Kara was still laughing at Larry. Now that was making her feel so much better that she was able to get Mr. Larry back at last for the way he had be treated her. For once I'm running in the big league now," said Kara.

"Oh yes, Kara. That will just make me so much happier to get a picture of you. So come on. Let the man take our picture right now, and you are taking a few pictures by yourself. So will I. Look, baby, we have a long time before it is time to go to dinner, but now if you get a little on the hungry side, we can always go up to the top deck and get something to eat. There is always food on the top deck. Also, we will be having our dinner at 7:00 p.m. with the captain. We have been seated at his table tonight," said Larry.

"Oh, that's so nice, but can't we return back to the room after we finish with the pictures, Larry? I could use a little nap before it's time for dinner. I need to relax a few hours."

Now the first night on the ship everything went on just fine. No one was disappointed at all. The next morning she was up early, walked out on the deck to look around the ship, and saw the ship was sailing around an island in the Pacific. No stop. They will be out in the sea for a few days. We meet a few people on the ship, but Larry was not too happy about hanging out with no one, just him and me. We stayed to ourselves like we were newly wedded, and a few people asked but we just smiled and keep on walking. Now all day, all I can see is water, no land. But now I had to give it to him. I do like this ship. We get in the pool or go do some exercise. Now we need to stretch our joints into action. The next day I needed some time to myself. Like some personal service from the beauty salon. My hair had started looking mighty bad. The day and night was all so beautiful. It was warm, dry, and at night there were no bad storms at all. Not so far. There was so much going on that you could never get lonesome. Nevertheless, my day is a challenge with Larry.

As he spoke, Larry wrapped his arms around Kara. She wanted to pull away from him, but she felt paralyzed by the strange feeling that had started stirring within her body.

"Let tonight be a very special night."

Kara could feel her heart thundering against her ribs. She was still looking at the moonlight playing across his handsome face.

"Kara, don't you have a kiss for me after all these day? You sure are comfortable with me by now my love."

Suddenly she felt his warm mouth briefly graze her cool lips, and something inside her just seemed to leap right out of her body. It had been six years since she had a man, and her body was on fire. She thought until now that she couldn't afford to lose her cool. She was gazing into the shadows of the oncoming darkness. The boat was moving far into the dark of the night. All I could see was the black of the night and a good-looking man asking me to make love to him tonight. I had to think it over. The old ghosts were too thick for me.

Larry's mood seemed to change like the night wind. Suddenly the increase of the wind rises. It builds up the wind and the water. Ridges swell moving along the surface making waves. You can't see the ocean stretching vast and dark laced with the burning reflections of the moon and the early stars. The sea is murmuring old eternal dreams in its sleep. My feeling for Larry is growing very deep.

"Larry, let's turn in early tonight."

"When do we start?" he asked.

"Right now," she whispered looking at him with a smile.

Without a backward glance, she and Larry walked into the room.

He closed the door behind them. Then he was beside her gathering her in his arms, his weight above her as he kissed her with an urgency which was both brutal and relentless. He called her name.

"Kara, oh Kara," he moaned as his lips burned over her mouth and against her hair, cupping her face as he forced her to look at him.

"Oh no, for God sake. Don't start crying. I can't bear it. Not now."

He brushed away her tears. She wasn't even certain why she was crying at all. She knew what she needed was this man right now.

She said very softly, "Make love to me, Larry."

He lifted his head up and looked at her. But she silenced his words with her finger and a smile. Right now the reason do it is matter at all. Her hand stroked his back, and her nails were digging into his well-developed, strong muscles. She could feel him shudder and tremble uncontrollably as she deliberately continued.

"Oh my, Kara. My God, woman, you are driving me right out of my mind," he said softly. "Kara, my love, what are you doing to me? I need you to know, my God, woman. I have been needing you ever since day one. Oh, Kara, never take your love away from me."

She knew from the throbbing and the sense of urgency that she held this man's power in spite of his physical male strength. At this moment, he was the most vulnerable.

Kara was like a crazy woman. She couldn't get enough of this man. His voice was hoarse as he drew her towards him. Now he was careful with her. He touched and stroked every part of her body. There was not a spot that he didn't touch. He molded her to him until it seemed they had become one. It had been so long since she engaged in sex that she was out of her mind. She wanted so much more, but she knew she had to be careful about this. She had to be concerned about his feelings and hers.

The next morning the ship docked for the day. The ship will remain at the island until 6 p.m. So, it looked like everybody had already gone their own separate way.

"Kara, let's take one of the taxis with the flap on the top. The one that is operated by licensed guides who can get you around the island and give a narrated touring at the same time. We can do a lot of sightseeing in the taxis. Then, we will do some walking down to the water. I would like to take you to the underwater exploration. Right now, we will do some touring of the Bermuda Islands. Look! The Royal Naval dock yards. We will start right here. The craft stores may have nice things in them, and at the clock tower mall you can get your gifts for your family."

"Next, we can visit the underwater exploration. Baby, the ocean comes to life. We can go diving 12,000 feet below sea level.

Kara, you will like it. Come, it's fun."
"Oh Larry, I have to get in that submarine and go down to the bottom of the sea. Oh, my Larry!"
"Well here we go, Kara. You can see the sharks in a cage. It's a lot of fun."
"Yes, Larry, you already said that. I can't swim or drink all this water. So, it's not fun to me. So let's get it over with right now, Larry. Okay? But you are not funny, my love."
She and Larry took the submarine to the bottom of the sea. Kara didn't see a thing. She had her eyes closed all the time. She came back up without getting wet. That makes her a little happier.
"Come on, Kara. I think you will like to see the treasures that were recovered from the shipwreck on the Bermuda shores. They are on display as well as some sea shells from around the world. You need to take a rest. Let's go to the pubs, or we can go to Tom Moore's Tavern at Bailey's Bay. That was built in 1652. It is the most fascinating tavern in Bermuda and the oldest eating place. Baby, this place has lots of history. It was named after this Irish poet. The man arrived here in 1804. The building was constructed by a shipwright. It's originally made of cedar. And the ribs are still visible. You know the tavern has five delightful dining rooms to eat at and a spacious outdoor patio that also overlooks the bay."
"So, come, my love, let's take the taxis and go to the tavern to eat," said Larry.
"Oh yes, man, let's do that. Just talking about food is making me hungry. Let's go right now. All this touring can work up a good appetite. All of a sudden I'm craving for some food."
The two took a taxi to go to the tavern. They walked into the dining room. You could smell the odor of food. As you walk through the door, it smelled so good. Now Bermudians love to socialize while you are have dinner. You can meet some of the locals at Tom Moore's Tavern at Bailey's Bay. It was built in 1652. This fascinating establishment is open daily for dinner. They also have live entertainment. The jazz band played some good music, and we overlooked the bay, too.
You could also enjoy the scents of the jasmine, the Easter Lilies, and the rosemary from the garden. Larry and Kara ordered crisp, roasted breast of duckling with duck comfits, spring roll with raspberry juice, vegetables, and wine with the meal. After dinner, the two did more sight seeing. The island offers a wealth of natural treasures to discover at Warwick Long Bay. Warwick, Shelley Bay, and also Hamilton Parish have pink beaches and aqua water. The Princess Hotel opened its doors in 1885 and is also known as the pink palace. It

overlooks the Harbor and is a five minute stroll to down town.
"Oh Larry, this is a very luxurious place with pink sand and the
Botanical Gardens. I have never seen so many beautiful flowers and
brightly colored blossoms. You never want to come out of the gardens."
"Oh, Larry, you know everything is so nice and beautiful.
Would you look at the large pool with the fresh water? Oh you know
something, Larry? I can swim now. A person like me who can't swim
can go in this here shallow pool. I can't see it is for the children, but
look than also have a luxury spa."
   "Oh right, my little Kara, you know it is getting to be that time
to take our taxi back to the ship. We do not need the ship to go and
leave us here on this Island. Kara you do know that we are a long way
for the ship, so do come on, my love. The taxi comes to meet them. He
took them back to the ship. The taxi man was so very nice to take them
all over the island in one full day. So Larry paid him very well. But
once Kara got in the taxis and sat down, she put her head on Larry's
shoulder and went to sleep. She was sleeping so good that Larry didn't
want to wake her, but he had to. They were back at the ship. Larry
called Kara so she could awaken. She became alert. She got out of the
taxi and walked into the ship with Larry and was heading straight to her
room. It was a nice day, but she was so tired and exhausted. She was
totally drained of all her strength and her energy.
   Now after a long day, Kara has had all the exercise she needs
right now. She wanted to get some rest and more sleep before it was
time to go down for dinner. She was not hungry. She had a good meal
at the tavern, so she was not hungry at all right now. But she couldn't
speak for Larry. He might want to go to dinner. Now he could have
been a nice man and go by himself and just leave her by herself. Kara
was not used to this long daydream. She was used to marching to her
own beat. She knew that Larry liked all this drama. But he didn't know
that poor Kara was a home body, not some drama queen like her two
best friends, Helen and Pam. Now those two would have loved all this
sight seeing and tours around the island all day. But poor me, I am so
tired right now. Like the old saying goes, when you're in the island, you
play the island rules. So come on, old girl, you got to keep yourself
under control at all times. So be nice, little girl, and put that big, old
smile on your face.

CHAPTER THIRTEEN

Kara walked into the sitting room and sat down and laid back with her eyes closed, almost sleep. Larry came into the room and looked at Kara.

He said, "Come on, my love, you look so beat. You could use some rest before dinner time. So come on, my love, and take a shower. In the mean time, I will order our dinner and have it brought to our room, okay? Look, love, I'm here to spoil you rotten at all times,"

He put Kara on her feet and put his arm around her and gave her a hug. He started to kiss her.

All of a sudden he stopped without warning, he just looked at her, and pushed her toward the bathroom saying, "Baby, take your shower. After that, you take a good rest. Get that shower and a beauty nap. It will sure make you feel better," said Larry.

"Oh, thank you, Larry. You are spoiling me, alright, and I love it."

"I will remove myself for you now."

"You know all that walking and sightseeing took its toll me. Oh, Larry, you know something? You are my knight in shining in my heart."

She kissed Larry on the lips and turned the shower on. As she stood under the water, she almost fell asleep. The hot water felt so good on her body. All she need right now was the bed and good night's sleep. But she knew that Larry had said something about a good band playing in the ballroom tonight. She also knew that she couldn't always take all of his fun, so she took a short nap and would be ready to go to the ballroom to dance the night away with a smile on her face. She laid her head down on the pillow and was out like a light. Larry looked in on Kara. She was already deep asleep before her head hit the pillow.

Larry looked at Kara, "Well, my love, I will take a shower, also."

But after his shower, he was going to check out the ship's casino. The ship was already out in the sea, so that meant everything was open for business. Now he can go and take in some good old gambling while Kara naps. Then she can't interfere with his playing cards. She needs rest, and he needs to gamble a little while she rests. He will go and play a few hands of Blackjack. Larry liked to play cards every chance he got which wasn't often. He doesn't like anyone to talk to him while playing cards. So, everything is turning out just right for him. Kara is resting nicely. Larry took his shower, dressed, and left the room.

Larry had been at the table for a few minutes and already won a game. He started out with a good hand. After an hour, he thought it was about time check on his woman. He picked up his winnings and cashed out his chips at the cashier's window. He headed back to the room to check on Kara. He opened the door and walked into the sitting room to find Kara ready to go out for the night.

Larry stopped and looked at her. Kara was looking darn good, too. He was kind of surprised to see her up and dressed. He thought that he would have to come back and wake her up, but, instead, he found his woman all up and dressed. It made his day.

He just loved a woman like that. He couldn't take a lazy person at all. Now a person like that can get his heart any day.

"Well, my love, did you get enough rest? Are you already to go out for the night? It looks like you are ready to step out with your man. My love, said Larry.

"Oh, yes, Larry, that little nap really help me out a lot. So now your woman is already just for you. My night is all yours for the taking. I'm all yours, my knight in shining armor."

Kara started to laugh. She was looking at Larry.

"Didn't you say something about you wanted to go out dancing tonight? Well, my love, your woman is all ready to go dance the night away. I even have on my dance shoes. I will try to keep you on the dance floor most of the night."

"Now, I like to dance. I can move on down the line. You did say you liked to dance, right?" asked Kara.

Larry was still looking at Kara. She was looking so good to him. She had put on one of Pam sexy, black dressed, a slimming one with an off the shoulder, two lengths neckline, long side slits in all the right places. She was one hot mom in that dress, and Larry could not take his eyes off her.

Larry said to Kara, "Look here, woman, I don't like the idea of taking you out to dance with you looking that good. All eyes will be on you."

I think I'm just trying to keep you right here in this room. You're too hot for me to touch. I might get burned! You're a hot mom. And to think someone else is looking at or touching you. I will just have to punch someone out."

Now he was laughing. He and Kara laugh.

Kara looked at Larry and said, "Oh you need to stop it, Larry. I'm all dressed up for your eyes only and no one else. Otherwise, where can I go? I'm with you now. And you will not push me overboard, so the next thing I can do is to go back to bed without you. Are with you?"

Now she was the one to have the last laugh.

"Oh my, Larry. You can be on the jealous side now can't you? My loved one, you know I have waited for six years. I will not let one night turn me into a hot mom and make me act like a big fool," said Kara.

"Alright, my Kara, I will be so nice and take it all back. But Kara, there is just one thing you just said. Now we can go to bed for some hot, sweet love.

And no sleep will come our way this night, my sweet, little Kara. I would just love to make all kinds of crazy love to you. I would stay right here right now, Ms. Kara. Do we have a deal? Because my mind is working a little overtime.

"Oh, Larry, will you get dressed. Let's eat and then head out to the dance. We will see about the fun times much later, my knight in shining armor."

Kara, do you still remember me warning you the first time I met you? I said that you could handle me, and I gave you a fair warning. It is not my fault that you decided not to take my heed," said Larry.

Kara looked at Larry with a grin, "How could I forget? I knew I was in a lot of trouble from day one when you warned me I might not be able to handle you. Also you know that life do not always turn out the way you want it to anyway. I never in a lifetime thought I would be on a ship with a man. To top it all off, I'm on this trip without my friends or family, and you talk about do I remember! Oh, yes, Mr. Larry, I do very well. Like everyday. How can I forget?" asked Kara.

"Oh, come on, my sweet, little woman. You are right on the ball since you got on this boat with me. Woman, you are all right in my book. Just don't change a thing about you. Look here, my woman. I will go and change my clothes, and we will be on the way to the dance."

The ballroom was overflowing with beautiful people of all ages. The Reggae rhythms blared, and people were rocking to the soulful beat.

"Oh, Larry, do you think we can get a table? It is mighty

crowded."

He was looking around and saw an empty table. He pointed at the only table in sight. They walked over to the table, sat down, and listened to the music.

"Kara, can you dance to this music? I love Reggae music. If you can, I would like to dance with you, my love. You did say you had on your dancing shoes. I would like to dance all night long because, woman, this is music that I can dance to the beat. First, let me order us a drink before we dance. I could use a good drink."

I want to see you shake your hips, my love. I'm all ready and hope you are ready for me, too. I know you can't satisfy me all the way, baby. Kara, I need you to rock my world and wrap me in all your love."

"Oh, Larry, I haven't got one clue what you are talking about right now, but I have no regrets. This week has been the best time of my life. I can't find any fault at all. This has been one of the best weeks of my life with you. Take my word for it, my love. Some strange thing is happening everyday. Keep on doing what you have been putting on me every minute. Ain't nothing like a good, old time. I think at last I found Mr. Right this time for good."

Kara made a silent oath to keep her head screwed on straight in the ballroom. The drinks came. She and Larry sat and looked at the other people for a little while and then got up to dance.

She was enjoying the dance now. Larry could really dance. He was moving so good on the floor. His body was moving like he was flying away from me. He had every nerve cell acting up again, and she was getting emotional.

"Boy, what's the matter with her?"

His body was moving so easy. She couldn't dance like her man. He has the floor right now. It looks like everybody had their eyes on him. Larry was in his own little world with a smile on his face.

"Larry, you said all the eyes were going to be on me, but I'm sorry to say, Larry, you took the eyes away for me. You took the show tonight. Every woman wants to dance with you.

Larry, you move your body so sexy. All the women were ready to take you to bed. Your body was building up all kinds of charm that was attracting us all. Anything connected with you and your sexual dance? So, Mr. Larry, I'm taking you out of this ballroom. If I don't, I will not have a man when tomorrow morning comes because somebody will have taken you away from me. Larry, do you also know that you are mine until we get of this boat. The way you dance you're so light on your feet as if the wind just lifted you up off the floor. You dance with the art of the dance of death, whirling a person away in a dance as each dies with a sexual look in their eyes.

Do you know that this kind of power is to influence and control others? Now you know, and I will not forget it. That was the sexiest dance that I had ever seen in my life time. We haven't known each other too long, but the time I had spent with you, we don't always need words to speak to one another. Nevertheless, I want to tell you that I cherish our deep friendship. Larry, this night do you know that you have touched my life in a million wonderful ways. What a blessing to have a good friend like you. It is so hard to find such a dear friend, and impossible to replace a good friend like you even though you know that you have influence over others, that great power to control oneself. So I would very much like to hold on to you a little bit longer. I am rejoicing with you, so Larry, my love, whatever you have been doing tonight, please don't stop. I get such a good feeling just looking at you. I want to try to dance all night myself. You have already proved that dreams can come true at the end when you believe in yourself. Now we have been on this ship for a week and you can believe I had a wonderful time."

"Oh, Larry, you do know you are a rare treasure. I just want to thank you for all you have done for me. I was drowning at the bottom of my own little world. Only you could have known exactly what would make me a different person out of me. Larry, I just want to thank you for knowing me a little better than I actually know myself. That's why you became my knight in shining armor! You came riding in on your white horse with a big smile on your face. You have restored my faith in a man, and I step right out in the world at last once and for all. There are no words to express my gratitude for all you have done for this woman along the way."

"Do you know something, Larry? Life didn't mean much to me at one time. You know something? I was a very lonesome person for a long time. I put all my life in my children and worked. I was trying so hard to take away a lot of things. I could not tell him to leave me. It hurt too bad. My father nicely asked him to get out of my life and to stay out. Larry, since I met you, things have changed so much. Without you as my friend, I do not think I would be the person that I am today," said Kara.

"My God, Kara. I didn't know that you could talk that much. Oh, my sweet woman. Yes, let's go out on the ship and get some fresh air. Are you getting a little tired? If so, we can go back to the room. It is so cool and refreshing. The fresh, strong winds flowing in from the sea, the night is black dark, no lights, and the only light was coming from the boat. No stars were shining at all tonight. He took her into his arms and started to kiss her. She was all in his world right now.

"Look, my love, let's go to the room. I need you right this minute. So can we make it to the cabin? Oh, Kara, I want you to flow for me, my darling, all night long. Will you satisfy me tonight? I'm all ready for you, woman and hope the same with you. Do I need to carry you to the cabin? If so, tell me now, or I will take you right up like a little baby."

He was laughing all the time walking to the elevator. He was right behind. The shoe was on the other foot. Larry was taking complete authority. She was not in control this time.

"Well, now, my little Kara. It is my turn to be the man," he breathed.

"You explained lots of things to me tonight that made me want you that much more than before."

"Oh Kara, you can stop running now."

"Oh Larry are you saying that you have regrets for what happened the other night?"

A tiny flicker of fear widened her eyes, and she heard him swear softly.

"Oh No! Hell no! Woman, I will prove to you that I have no regrets at all with you."

He took her in his arms and started kissing her. He took her face and looked in her eyes. His hands tilted her head up so she could look at him.

"You are one in a million, angel. Oh, Kara, do you actually know how special you are to me? I never want you to be afraid of me."

He kissed her lips softly to show her how much he really cared for her.

"Where have you been all my life?" asked Larry.

She looked at Larry and said, "It seems like I've have been running or hiding from you, and getting disappointed by one man. But, Larry, tonight I just want to hideaway in your arms. So will you make a woman out of me this night?"

Larry put his arms around her and stuck his tongue in her mouth delighting in the sweetness of her. She moved on him and continued to send him to unparalleled heights. His hand moved across her backside gently as he caressed her, and then moved steadily across her skin until he parted her legs as Kara rubbed against his swollen member. Larry arched his hips and moved them sensuously. Then he placed two fingers into her love canal. She climaxed yet again screaming out his name as the feel of him pressed against her love button. Combined with his gentle touch, he drove her to the breaking point. It had been so long for her. The first time he touched her it was so fast and quick and over with but this time he was making her feel like a virgin.

"Kara, I want to feel you. I want to feel you. Oh, you are ready for me this time," he was moaned.

"Oh yes, hell yes! Larry, I want you to make love to me," she was said in a tiny voice.

He turned her over gently so that she was now on her back. He reached inside the dresser and grabbed out a condom.

He looked at Kara and asked her would she like to put it on for him. He was kneeling over her. Kara took the condom from him and placed it on his penis. She opened her legs wanting to feel all of him this time.

"Oh, baby, I will take my time, whispered" lowering his head and kissing her hungrily. Nibbling at her neck and ear caused her to move her hips underneath him in anticipation of what was to come. In the next seconds, Larry took his manhood in his hand and guided it to her opening.

"Tell me, baby, if I'm hurting you, and I will stop," he said breathlessly.

The feel of her moist lips against the head of his penis was so delicious that he grunted uncontrollably. He was trying so hard to push slowly and felt her cushiony softness giving way for him to enter in her. Kara seemed to be holding her breath at the feel of his manhood at the door of her secret garden. She was a little tense. It was hurting, but, hell, it felt so good to her.

"Oh, baby, please relax, my baby. I need you to relax," he urged.

Larry continued to push and was intoxicated by the reality of becoming a part of her.

Boy, she is so tight, but that was to be expected. She was warm and so wet. She was also driving him insane. He was a little on the surprised side when she arched her hips up to allow him more leverage, and, before he knew it, he was completely inside of her.

"Oh, Larry! Oh, oh, Larry," she yelled breathlessly.

He felt as if he would explode in her any second. He could not believe just how good she felt. She was moving against him slowly. Oh no, he loved every second of it, but hell the end was about to come.

"Oh wait! Wait baby, don't move, please don't move."

He didn't was to come now, not now. He was moaning in her ear, "Not yet." But he had never felt any thing so good in his life before. Oh this sensation caused him to fill her up. The way he was felt, he pushed that last time. She had come up to meet him halfway! Although it was very uncomfortable at first, she knew the moment he was completely inside of her.

She was already in her own little world against. She was trying to tighten every muscle that she had in her body. She didn't want that good feeling to ever stop. This here man was working all kinds of sexual pleasure. He is one sex machine, and a good one, too. Now that man who called himself my husband only the managed his home but not his sex affairs at home. He was too busy running after other women. She moved against him slowly loving the feel of his hard body mingling with hers. She could not stop her body from moving. She was having another orgasm. She called his name over and over again. He held her tightly. He was not quite ready to give up, not right now. So he began to stroke her with a new fervor. But she met him with every thrust for thrust. They made love with reckless abandon.

Larry loved the way she let her body meet his. Kara was happier than she had ever been in her life. She began to cry. She was so overcome with emotion that she could not help herself for feeling this way. Larry just held her and climaxing with her this time. Their love making calmed. For a long time, she just lay in his arms so exhausted yet so cheerful. It was only when she turned to look at him thinking that he had already fallen asleep. She realized that he was studying her at will. His dark eyes were taking in every part of her body. Her naked body was glowing in the dark. She felt herself shiver with excitement as he turned towards her again. Kara had never believed that this could be possible. She was lying in a bed with a man, just naked, and loved it even though she still felt a little drugged. And yet pleasure filled her up from that first sweet sensuous wild night filled with delight. So fantastic, it was the best love making she had ever had.

Now you not alone woman without a man. Six years sure can make you do some weird ass things to your body and mind. Now I have been doing thing that I have never in my life done with the man I will be wedding. Like they always say, you make your bed so you lie in it. Hell I try, but it didn't work out. We walked down the wrong road or did I just have the wrong man in the first place. He was complaining that I was the wrong woman. We didn't even fit right together in bed or out bed. Now it seems he wasn't even a sexy man in my book. Now Larry is rocking my world. He is Mr. Right. He looks at me with his sexy, dark eyes with a smile on his face with the hot ass sexual look. He drew her much closer to him. She was feeling that strange man power that controls over her life right now. In one swift movement, he had her pinned beneath him, and this time there was no doubt about his superiority. He was making all kinds of love to her right now. This man is just taking over her body.

It wasn't even her anymore. He was a man that just took complete authority. He had already said to her that there was no turning back in his book at all. Boy, this man became the body taker," said Kara.

"Well, my sweet woman, it is my turn to run this show. Don't go any further," he breathed very hard look at her. "Kara, you going to explain to me a lot of things about yourself. I look at you sometimes, and your mind is somewhere else. Yes, your body is still with me, but your mind and soul are a long way from here. You have been looking out to the sea looking so sad, baby. What can I do to make you happy again? Hell, Kara, I have been wanting you for a long time, baby. I need you to stop that running now. I just need to know that you are not going to up and disappear like some beautiful butterfly the minute I let you out of my sight. You know, my sweet Kara, if you decide to leave me I will hire my future son to be my lawyer and get you back."

"Into my waiting arms, my love. Kara, if I had known that you really cared for me this much, hell, baby, you know something? We didn't need to come on this cruise. We could be home making some wilder crazy love."

Her body was acting up, yes, like crazy, right now. She was smiling at Larry, "Oh Larry, you have to understand when we were at home there was no thrill, but right now all the thrill is here. The open sea has helped me open my eyes to a lot of things that I have to think twice before I made this trip with you. And I hope that we both are glad that we are here together."

Kara was breathing hard. She needed him again.

"Oh, Larry, I won't disappear from you."

She told him with a husky voice.

"I realized that you were right when you said that I can't keep on running forever. Suddenly, I had to face reality one day."

She swallowed hard as tears threatened to well up in her eyes for a lone, tense moment he just looked down at her before sliding down beside her.

Kissing away her tears, "Kara, look baby, I know I have said a lot of things to you that I had no right to say to you at all, my love."

She put her arms out and drew his head toward her breast.

"Oh, my Kara, you do know that you are my little, spring flower. One day you will be Mrs. Grant. But first I have to ask your father for your hand. Your whole family knows that I love you. They do not keep secret. So will you marry me, Kara, and keep me out of trouble."

THE END

About the Author: Cara Williams

Cara Williams was born and raised in a Christian home located in a small rural town in northern North Carolina. Reading at 10 years old, she enjoys reading good mystery books. She enjoys dancing and singing with the gospel group that she manages.

Printed in the United States
137562LV00002B/11/P

9 780981 688343